MERA NAAM JOKER

Khwaja Ahmad Abbas (1914–1987) is considered one of the pioneers of Indian parallel or neo-realistic cinema. He was a film-maker, novelist, screenwriter and a journalist in Urdu, Hindi and English, who preferred to call himself a communicator. As a film-maker, he directed award-winning films like *Dharti Ke Lal* (1946), *Pardesi* (1957), *Shehar Aur Sapna* (1963), *Saat Hindustani* (1969), and *Do Boond Pani* (1972), among others. As a screenwriter, K.A. Abbas wrote films like *Neecha Nagar* (1946) and *Jaagte Raho* (1956), which won international awards. Apart from this, he scripted some of the best films of Raj Kapoor, creating the immortal tramp in *Awara* (1951) and *Shree 420* (1955). He also wrote the screenplays of *Mera Naam Joker* (1969), *Bobby* (1973) and *Henna* (1991). His column, 'Last Page', holds the distinction of being one of the longest-running columns in the history of Indian journalism. He published seventy-three books in English, Urdu and Hindi, including an engaging autobiography, *I Am Not an Island*, and two semi-autobiographical novels, *Inquilab* and *The World Is My Village*. He was awarded the Padma Shri in 1969.

Suresh Kohli is a poet, writer, translator, editor, literary critic and film historian with more than twenty-five published works. He is also a short and documentary film-maker, with over a hundred films to his credit. He lives in Delhi.

MERA NAAM JOKER

The Complete Story

KHWAJA AHMAD ABBAS

Edited and with an Introduction by

SURESH KOHLI

HarperCollins *Publishers* India

First published in 1970 by Hind Pocket Books

This edition published in India by
HarperCollins *Publishers* in 2014

4th Floor, Tower A, Building No. 10, Phase II,
DLF Cyber City, Gurugram, Haryana -122002
www.harpercollins.co.in

4 6 8 10 9 7 5 3

ISBN: 978-93-5029-623-3

Typeset in 14/14.4 Adobe Arabic
Jojy Philip New Delhi 110 015

Printed and bound at
MicroPrints India, New Delhi

To

The Joker who lives within the heart of Raj Kapoor

CREDITS

Cast

Rajoo (The Joker):	Raj Kapoor
David:	Manoj Kumar
Mary:	Simi Garewal
Young Rajoo:	Rishi Kapoor
Mahender:	Dharmendra
Sher Singh:	Dara Singh
Marina:	Kseniya Ryabinkina
Meena:	Padmini
Kumar:	Rajendra Kumar
Rajoo's Mother:	Achala Sachdev
Member of the Soviet State Circus:	Eduard Sjereda

Crew

Directed, produced and edited by Raj Kapoor

Story and screenplay:	K.A. Abbas
Music:	Shankar–Jaikishan
Lyrics:	Shailendra, Hasrat Jaipuri, Neeraj, Prem Dhawan
Cinematography:	Radhu Karmakar
Art Direction:	M.R. Achrekar

INTRODUCTION

The idea of *Mera Naam Joker* first struck Raj Kapoor after he watched a Czechoslovakia State Circus show in Bombay on an early February night in 1960. The very next day, he approached his favourite scriptwriter, Khwaja Ahmad Abbas. In Raj Kapoor's own words: 'It is the story of a tear and a smile. It is the story of a character, the joker, who says, "I shall drink your tears and in return make you smile."' The statement was duly reproduced in the trade broadsheet *Screen* issue of 10 February.

The film released exactly a decade later (8 December 1970), seven years after the monumental hit, *Sangam* (in which Raj Kapoor had already begun to show signs of wear and tear). By now, Raj Kapoor the actor, though barely forty-six years old, had lost both shape and looks, and was clearly no longer acceptable as a hero. *Mera Naam Joker* was nearly five years in the making, and had Rajendra Kumar, Dharmendra,

Manoj Kumar, Dara Singh and Simi Garewal in supporting roles, and a plump Padmini as the heroine. Though an unmitigated box-office disaster, it managed five *Filmfare* trophies: Best Director (Raj Kapoor), Best Music (Shankar–Jaikishan), Best Cinematography (Radhu Karmakar), Best Sound Recordist (Allauddin) and Best Playback Singer (Manna Dey).

According to the grapevine, the original script had six segments, each with a different leading lady, and was proposed as two different films, each consisting of three chapters or sections. Though there seem to have been second thoughts, it does appear plausible, and looking at the speed and manner in which the film begins, it probably began that way. Manoj Kumar's name as a co-scriptwriter in the credit titles justifies his claim of rewriting the first part with the young joker. This was on the night of 24 October 1961—before Raj Kapoor began *Sangam*.

In the *Screen* issue of 4 December 1970, the main writer, Khwaja Ahmad Abbas was quoted as saying: 'I remember the occasion very well when, accompanied by friend and collaborator V.P. Sathe, with whom I like to discuss most of my screenplays, I took the finished script to Raj Kapoor. It was characteristic of him that he cancelled all appointments, gave strict instructions to the studio telephone operator that he was not to be disturbed. He had a bath, changed, burned incense before the various gods (and goddesses?) installed in his cottage, and only then he sat down to take in his hands the fat volume I presented to him. Raj respects his writers, and he respects their scripts, and he also takes pains to make this evident.

'The first script of *Awara* had been written like a short story. The script of *Shree 420* was written like a novella, or a long short story. But when it came to *Mera Naam Joker*, I gave him a leather-bound, two-hundred-page-long tome. Perhaps he dramatized a little, for instance, when he placed the bound volume on his head, as if it was a scripture, but I think for the moment he was entirely sincere. He has said it again and again that the script is a holy book for him, for it is the source of all his inspiration.'

It was his most ambitious venture and, technically, the country's most perfect film until then. And it was special as it was also supposedly autobiographical. But a lot went wrong during the making. According to his friend, publicist and producer, the late Bunny Reuben: 'During the course of the nine years it took Raj Kapoor to make *Mera Naam Joker*—of which full five years, 1965–70, were spent in actual production—the script got revised several times. New situations were added, earlier ones condensed, and dialogue was written, rewritten and again written to suit the innumerable stars as and when they were ready to enter the footage of this three-in-one blockbuster.'

In *Raj Kapoor: The Fabulous Showman*, grandiosely subtitled *An Intimate Biography*, quoting Abbas, Reuben elaborates: 'When we went to Raj's farm at Loni, near Poona, to revise the First Chapter introducing the young Raju (played by Chintu), Raj had a number of recollections of his own schooldays which he wanted incorporated in the scenes. We had planned a ten-day working schedule. After the first evening's session when Raj talked nostalgically about his boyhood experiences, I knew exactly what he wanted. When two people have been working together over a period of years and have acquired a regard for each other's capabilities, and have come to understand each other's viewpoints, a sixth sense begins to operate between them. Then work is no longer drudgery, changes are not irksome, suggestions are welcomed, even anticipated, and met halfway. A kind of telepathy informs one what the other wants.

'The scenes were recast and rewritten, entirely to his satisfaction, in just three days, and we came back a week before we were expected in Bombay ... Raj

Kapoor has the reputation of being the Great Lover, but few people realize that his one great, abiding and permanent love is film-making to which he will, and he does, subordinate everything else in the world. The time, the attention, the concern, that other people lavish on their families, children and friends, Raj Kapoor bestows on his films. Like all lovers, he is alternately nervous and overconfident, generous and jealous, large-hearted and possessive, overpowering and cringing, gentle and sadistic. Creation is a lonely process and very few people know how many lonely hours Raj Kapoor spends locked in his cottage, worrying how his "beloved", the film, is shaping up.

'While no great ideologue, Raj Kapoor is not allergic to ideas. Indeed, with his basic sympathy for the cause of the common man, he is more amenable to socially progressive ideas and humanist ideals, so long as their presentation does not interfere with the popularity potential of his film … uncanny mastery over the box office, the intuitive grasp of what will appeal to the public, his subtle way of weaving in music as an integral part of the narrative, his almost unequalled ability to purvey popular entertainment without pandering to the popular bad taste. It makes him—and his films—a uniquely powerful and potent medium for the transmission of ideas.'

But, in retrospect, this very overconfidence, this overindulgence determined the fall of *Mera Naam Joker* and, after a brief hiatus in the form of *Bobby*, returned in another disaster, *Satyam Shivam Sundram*. Coming back to *Joker*, the unchecked enthusiasm, the overindulgence resulted in the three chapters eventually becoming three full-length feature films. Abbas feared this would happen because Raj Kapoor made sure he was on hand for every shooting schedule, and was even made to direct a part of the circus procession sequence that was canned on the streets of Mumbai, attracting a huge multitude.

In *Raj Kapoor Speaks* (Penguin Viking, 2002), drawing from different sources, daughter Ritu Nanda quotes her father with regard to his association with Abbas and the making of the magnum opus: 'Has anybody seen my heart …? This scene from *Mera Naam Joker*, at the very beginning of the film, affects me deeply. The performer, the Joker, has invited all his past attachments, all those he has been emotionally involved with. He is giving his last performance because he has a premonition that he is going to die …

'I feel that we (artists) are the fortunate few in this

world who have had the boon of people looking into our hearts … of having loved them, and receiving love in return. This affects me tremendously.

'How different everything becomes as the perspective changes! Years ago, when *Mera Naam Joker* was only a monumental "literary scenario" written by K.A. Abbas, I used to browse through it, and I was almost frightened at the prospect of filming it! The whole canvas of it was so vast and compelling, the panorama of the world of entertainment and entertainers spreads limitlessly in this saga, the entire spread is so mighty, that it took me some time to absorb it.'

As a film-maker, Raj Kapoor was notorious for overshooting and, in this ambitious venture, he lost all count and calculation. He had a fixed image of a tramp, what all he embodies, what all he goes through while attempting to make the world laugh. So while he was busy collecting newer experiences, conjuring up images, the expanse of the film continued to assume gigantic proportions. 'The character of Joker embodies all that is spiritual and selfless … From his childhood to his death, the Joker moves from one phase of his life to the next. The different women that he loves leave the scars of separation and unfulfilled love on his heart. But the smile is always there on his lips. Concealing his tears, he goes about his mission in life to make people happy, to spread laughter and joy in the lives and hearts of young and the old alike.'

No one has been able to access the real Raj Kapoor, then or now. He carried within himself a multitude of masks, and sported one according to the demands of the situation. Behind the façade of humility lurked a highly opinionated persona, a vindictive human being. It is doubtful if he ever analysed his own actions. He was god-fearing and deeply religious, and at the same time selfish and self-centred. He was never wrong but always the wronged one. It is generally said that a man's ego should not be bigger than his balls, but Raj Kapoor carried his ego on his left sleeve. When he wanted something, he would succumb to any low, or indulge in any form of flattery to achieve his ends. One hasn't really heard of any of his acts of generosity except in his devotion to his art. There was no scope for any compromises. Especially when he was making a film.

With everything at his beck and call, what really went wrong? Different theories have been propounded, discussed and debated over the decades. According to Bunny Reuben, 'The film ... should have been a film about a young man who wants to become a circus clown and does. Then he falls in love with a Russian trapeze-girl and eventually she goes back to Russia, leaving him broken-hearted—yet the eternal clown. In other words, the full film should have been that second part alone. If this was so, all that scintillating footage depicting the various animals and clown routines as well as so many breathtaking trapeze stunts which had been shot but which had perforce to be taken out in order to bring down the length of the circus chapter and make it compatible with the three-in-one format, could have remained in the film—and I think it would then have always ranked as India's greatest circus film of all time.

'The first part should have been an independent film about a sensitive schoolboy who experiences first love and sexual awakening by falling in love with his teacher. The film, about eight to nine thousand feet long, could have held its own as a festival entry anywhere and, in the domestic market, being a Raj Kapoor film, it would have been a runner too. As a matter of fact, Raj's second son, Rishi, whom the showman introduced in this chapter as the awkward schoolboy, won the National Award as Best Child Actor for his performance in the film. And the last chapter? It should never have been made at all.'

Rishi Kapoor recalls how he got to know he would

be in the film, and his initial reaction. 'I was having dinner when Papa came home, and spoke to my mother. He said, "Krishna (that's my mother), do you mind if I cast Chintu as a teenage Raj Kapoor in the film?" Mom said, "Well, I have no objection as long as he does not miss school and his studies are not affected." I listened to all this very attentively without giving the impression that I was doing so. I finished dinner, went to my room, washed my hands and went to the study table, opened a notebook from the drawer and scribbled my signature.'

Back to Reuben: 'It is interesting to note that by the time the shooting of *Joker* was nearing its end Raj Kapoor had realized that it was not the laugher-filled film he had set out to make. *Mera Naam Joker* was always supposed to be a comedy, a sparkling, fun-filled story of a clown who makes the world laugh, and the laughter and fun were to be a camouflage for the real pathos and tragedy which lay beneath. The film as it had taken shape, however, was lugubrious and weepy. Desperately seeking to inject some laughter into the footage, Raj asked veteran Hollywood-trained make-up man Sarosh Mody to bring in Adi Marzban, the well-known writer of Parsi stage comedies, to write comedy for the film. It was too late, however. It was impossible to "inject" comedy into the already completed footage. For that, the film would have had to be re-scripted and re-shot.'

Let's take a look at what Abbas, the writer, has to say about the end product, as it appeared in the *Screen* issue of 4 December 1970: 'Frankly, there are aspects of Raj Kapoor's personality that I do not like, at least I do not understand them. Sometimes he is vain, temperamental, irresponsible, impossible … It is again characteristic of our peculiar relationship that when it came to economizing on footage in the final stages of editing, it was Raj Kapoor who was jealously guarding any manhandling of my key dialogues, and it was I who was protesting—"over my dead body"—against any attempt to cut any of the scenes in which Raj Kapoor, the great thespian, had excelled himself … Actually, there was a babble of editing suggestions, and Raj patiently listened to all, and then, within the privacy of the cottage, he discussed them with me. I remember telling him, "Raj, listen to everyone but do as your mind and heart dictate. There is only one picture—*Mera Naam Joker*—and there is only one director: Raj Kapoor. Ultimately, it is his responsibility. Do as he tells you!"

'And that's exactly what he did, and all of us were amazed at the creative, constructive, transformation he achieved by the use of his editing scissors. When

I saw the finished film (though I had already seen it a dozen times during various stages of completion) I spontaneously started applauding with all the others when it ended—forgetting for the moment that I, too, had a little hand in its creation. It is not often that a writer feels that way about a picture and its maker, but when he does, he wants to proclaim it from house-tops.'

Various reasons have been expounded to explain the reasons for the film's failure, including implausible trade manipulations by rival sections. No amount of manipulation can cause *such* damage to a film, especially when it was a Raj Kapoor creation, an autobiographical one at that. For had there been even an iota of truth to these allegations, *Sangam*, the film before *Joker*, or *Bobby* that followed it, would not have been such colossal hits. The audience waited with bated breath to watch Raj Kapoor's magnum opus. But what it saw belied its monumental expectations. Let's look at what the great showman had to say:

'When people ask me why I made *Mera Naam Joker* and how I thought I could contain such mighty dimensions of a saga-like script within the frame of a motion picture, I smile to myself and remember my school days—the innumerable clowns I had seen on screen, old friends like Charlie Chaplin, the

Marx Brothers, Buster Keaton, Joe E. Brown, Laurel and Hardy, and many more, the circuses I had watched, the innumerable half-forgotten clowns I had laughed at and with, the trapeze girls and the funny performing animals. And through all this panorama of laughter, I remember the single tear in the little clown's eye. The soul of the universe is contained in a laugh and a tear and I have vibrated to both through a crowded, intense and fully lived life.

'To make such an immense film, to be able to put on the screen all that imagination can conceive and conjure up, is no easy task, and the making of *Mera Naam Joker* was fraught with gigantic problems. All these could be and were tackled on a larger-than-life scale. Gorgeous sets were conceived and erected with no consideration to cost. Amazing visual effects of forced perspective and optical illusions were imagined and then we went ahead and made all our imaginings into reality.

'My film *Mera Naam Joker* flopped. All the people who had worked with me and been by my side, and who had earned millions and millions of rupees from my films, turned their back on me. R.K. Studio, my house, my wife's jewellery … everything that I could see was mortgaged! I thought I was finished. Then I looked up and saw that famous R.K. banner and realized that everything is mortgaged but for the name "Raj Kapoor"—and as long as the banner is there, Raj Kapoor will be there. And I am sure that banner will be there always, shining as it shines today.'

The banner is there, but only in the form of a studio. *Henna* (1991), another ambitious venture that Raj Kapoor had been in the process of launching, was eventually directed by elder son Randhir Kapoor, and failed to muster support at the box office. *Prem Granth* (1996), directed by youngest son Rajiv Kapoor, also bit the dust. After a hiatus, even Rishi Kapoor, having retired as a romantic hero, tried his hand at direction with *Aa Ab Laut Chalen* (1999). After this, too, met a similar fate, there has been no attempt by the brothers to revive the famous banner, nor does there seem to be any hope of it being revived despite occasional flutters to the contrary.

'Jeena yahaan, marna yahaan / iske siwa jaana kahaan / jee chaahe jab hum ko awaaz do / hum hai wahin hum the jahaan.' This is what the joker sang, leaving behind an unforgettable legacy.

If I recall correctly, I met Raj Kapoor after a huge gap some time towards the end of 1985 at the Devnar Cottage in Chembur after a sneak preview of his last directorial venture, *Ram Teri Ganga Maili*, to which I had been specially invited along with Abbas and Sathe saheb. I was spellbound by what I saw though it was yet without a beginning and an end. I had been staying with Abbas saheb those days and had been dragged into a discussion about a plausible beginning and end. We were driven to the bungalow after the screening at the R.K. Preview Theatre in the studio complex. A literal darbar was already in place, with copious amounts of liquor flowing.

As usual, Abbas saheb declined the generous offer of cognac, saying, 'Suresh will give you company.' And I did, until dinner was served. I could not contain myself, when Raj-ji asked me about the screening, and blurted out: 'This is going to be your biggest hit.' Expanding his already formidable chest, he shouted, 'Krishna-ji … arre, Krishna-ji ko bulao.' When the lady of the house came hurrying in, he said, 'Listen to what this young man is saying and you always taunt me that I am either sleeping or drinking.' He made me repeat what I had said.

When some months later we went to see the final cut, and later drove to Devnar, Raj Kapoor was too sick to join the crowd. He had been unhappy with the 'happy' ending, which was not what he wanted, but which he had been pressurized into executing. The film, his parting gift to his audiences, indeed became a blockbuster.

I last exchanged greetings with him on a rather sad and sombre occasion, the burial of Khwaja Ahmad Abbas on 1 June 1987. Raj Kapoor did not live long thereafter, and left the mortal world exactly a year later.

Mera Naam Joker might have been a box-office disaster on its release, but is believed to be the most frequently watched Hindi movie on the video circuit.

New Delhi **SURESH KOHLI**
10 February 2014

Prologue

THE MASK AND THE MAN

1

A huge drum, with the laughing face of a clown painted on it, was being beaten to the rhythm of a circus band.

The blue dunce's cap with little golden bells dangling from the top of it, the cheeks red like a pair of ripe tomatoes, all the teeth on display in a wide, wild grin—but there was sadness, too, in the baby-blue eyes.

The clown-face—eternally grinning away at the world, even while the hammer-blows of the drumsticks pounded his cheeks, punched his nose, hit him in the eyes—was a symbol and more than a symbol. He was the Eternal Joker, and the harder he was hit, the more he was punched, the severer the blows of fate he received, the louder and merrier was the laughing rhythm that bounced out of the drum. This was the face not of any clown, but of a special clown, the Joker so many had once known and laughed at—and loved! On the banners being carried behind the drum, in the circus procession, were painted words that proclaimed an occasion for great joy—and great sorrow:

ONCE AGAIN HE COMES!
RAJOO
THE SINGING CLOWN
POSITIVELY LAST PERFORMANCE

The mile-long circus procession was wending its way through the main streets of Bombay.

There were elephants, horses, cages on wheels in which restlessly moved lions, tigers, leopards, bears, gorillas and monkeys, resenting the ogling eyes of the multitude.

Athletic gymnasts making spectacular somersaults even as they marched …

Shapely trapeze girls in tights carrying colourful flags and banners.

A motley crowd of clowns and jokers—tall jokers, pigmy jokers, fat jokers, thin jokers, all in their loud, funny costumes and comically painted faces—was marching in a hilariously disorderly manner, tripping each other, falling, vaulting, somersaulting, laughing and making the spectators laugh.

While everything in the procession was designed to be eye-catching and engaging, all eyes were focused on the banners and placards announcing the performance of Rajoo, the legendary clown who had retired from the circus years ago, and was staging a comeback just for one last performance. On the placards were painted the once familiar features of Rajoo who, years ago, had made millions laugh. But what they knew was not a man but a mask, an amusing puppet in a funny, loose-fitting costume, a clown–doll for the amusement of children. No one recognized the real, human face beneath the laughing mask. Was he gay or sad, young or old, a clumsy fool or a compassionate philosopher?

One such clown–doll was being taken out of a parcel by a grey-haired Christian lady, who was visibly shaken by the sight of the little joker. A strangely familiar music seemed to come floating out of her heart—or her past?—and brought a smile to that withered but beautiful face. Her sunken eyes glowed with sudden happiness. With the doll were two circus tickets and a letter and, while reading it, the old lady heard a fifteen-year-old schoolboy's voice:

> Madam, I am appearing in the last performance—the final exam—of my life. I will not trouble my teacher again. Please do come.
>
> Rajoo

Thousands of miles away, across the frozen Himalayas, in the revolutionary Red city of Moscow, on the seventeenth floor of a skyscraper on Prospekta Lenina, a uniformed messenger was ringing the doorbell.

A slim, middle-aged but beautiful blonde woman opened the door and, signing the receipt, took the parcel and a letter from the postman. She opened the parcel and took out the little clown-doll, which brought a smile to the severely handsome face and a flood of memories, tender and gay, of a faraway land. She recalled a familiar Indian voice as she read the letter:

> Marina, my friend, *moi lubov*,
> Even after so many years, I hope you still remember India and an Indian joker—'Klon' as you used to say—who presented his first performance in your presence. Won't you come to India to witness his last? They say thousands of miles separate Bombay from Moscow—but it takes only a few hours by jetplanes which were invented just for people who love one another!
>
> Raj-Joker

Back in Bombay, it was ten in the morning when the still glamorous but fading film star (who was no longer so young or so beautiful or so popular) opened her puffed-up eyes to greet a new day. The maidservant brought a tray containing her breakfast and the morning mail. Hot water with lime juice, brown bread without butter, and black, sugarless coffee—she shuddered at the sight of her slimming diet but prepared to endure it. Sipping the hot water, she opened the letter on top of the pile, and read:

> Believe me, Miss Meena, since I saw your last picture you have become my dream girl. I have simply fallen in love with you. Will you please send me an autographed photograph?

'All lies!' she said and threw back the letter in the pile, took a sip of bitter coffee to get over the taste in her mouth, and muttered all the time, mechanically opening another packet. 'There was only one person who loved me and, long ago, I lost him!'

Just then, out of the coloured tissue paper emerged the clown-doll, and the wrinkled film star embraced the little fellow like a long-lost sweetheart. With the doll was an envelope containing two circus tickets and a letter. Silently reading it, she heard a voice that seemed to come out of the past:

> Meena, my dear—or would you prefer me to call you 'Minoo Master'? I am presenting my

> farewell show—there will not be another. Will you come? Can you come? Do you even remember my name?
>
> Rajoo

Tears welled up in her eyes from which the old sparkle was gone and, as she looked at the doll, she felt the little Joker was laughing, though there was infinite sadness in those baby-blue eyes.

One little Joker sat on the glass top of the dressing table, ogling with unseeing blue-glass eyes at the Joker who sat in front of him.

The Joker, watching himself in the triple mirrors, was putting on make-up after many years, and so it took him a long time. Age, pain, sorrow and mortal sickness had left their marks and his face was furrowed with tiny lines. There were dark hollows under the eyes. But tonight he was determined not to be defeated by Time. Today, before his audience, he would be the young man they had known and applauded and loved.

With loving care, he applied foundation, greasepaint, rouge and powder. He applied the lipstick generously, elongating and enlarging his lips. The blue eyes were edged with mascara. There was a false, round, clown's nose fitted to his own original aquiline nose. And now, ready, he examined the three Jokers who peered at him from the triple mirrors.

Joker! Joker! How many Jokers?

One Joker was smiling.

The second Joker was laughing.

The third Joker was crying.

Smiling Joker!

Laughing Joker!

Weeping Joker!

Which was the real face of the Joker?

He was still pondering the imponderable when his old friend, Mahender, who was the owner of the circus, and an ex-trapeze artist, entered his tent. He was greying at the temples but still retained his trim, athletic body and his rugged good looks. The Joker thought that his friend had come to offer him his good wishes for this farewell performance, to encourage and inspire him. But Mahender seemed upset about something, and declared loudly: 'Rajoo, I am going to cancel your show tonight.'

On the made-up face of a clown, you can never see signs of surprise, astonishment, disappointment, anger, sorrow or pain. The lines painted on his face give him only one expression—whatever he may feel, the Joker is always laughing!

The Joker called Rajoo asked, 'Why?'

'Because,' Mahender exploded, 'the doctor has told me everything. You have a dangerously enlarged rheumatic heart, plus defective valves so that your heart gets only one-fifth of the normal blood supply. If you strain it by performing tonight, your heart may fail any moment. Sorry, Rajoo, I simply won't allow you to commit suicide.'

Rajoo the Joker got up from his stool and, slowly, smilingly, walked up to Mahender. 'All right. You can cancel my programme.' But hardly had Mahender reacted with satisfaction than Rajoo's next sentence completely bowled him over. 'But there is one condition. You will have to guarantee that if I don't perform tonight, I won't die—not tonight, not tomorrow, not after a year!'

Mahender was left speechless by the devastating logic of Rajoo's argument. With a sigh and a smile, he embraced Rajoo and said, 'You win and I lose. You shall perform tonight. The circus is at your disposal.'

'Thank you, Mahender Saheb!'

'Years ago I told you that my name is not Mahender Saheb, it's just plain and simple Mahender.'

'Yes, I remember, Mahender Saheb.'

'Again Saheb?'

'Yes, Saheb—No, Saheb!'

Between them it was an old, old gag and Mahender had a hearty laugh. 'You are a clown, Rajoo. You will never change—thank heavens.' Then he added in a more sombre tone, 'At least let me call a heart specialist—just in case!'

'Don't you worry, Mahender Saheb. I have called quite a few of my personal physicians.' Then he added with a sad and wry smile, 'You may even call them heart specialists.'

The circus was filled to capacity that night. All the tickets were sold out. But there were a dozen seats in the front row, kept reserved for Rajoo's special guests.

When the grey-haired Mary, wearing her Sunday best, came leaning on the arm of her husband, David, they were welcomed on behalf of Rajoo by Sher Singh, the former strongman and ringmaster, and now the manager of the circus. He led them to their reserved seats, and withdrew after making them comfortable. The circus ring was still empty and desolate, as the show would begin only after some minutes. So David lighted his cheroot and started blowing smoke rings in the air, but Mary's myopic eyes, through steel-rimmed spectacles, searched everywhere for Rajoo.

When the Russian Marina came, she was cordially greeted by Mahender. It seemed they were old friends and colleagues. Mahender led her to the seat next to Mary and David, and then, after a polite enquiry if she had a pleasant flight, he left. This circus was not unfamiliar to Marina, but her beautiful brown eyes were looking for Rajoo, who was nowhere to be seen. Had she made a mistake in coming all the way from Moscow?

There was a commotion at the entrance and Mahender ran in that direction. Was it a stampede of gatecrashers? No, it was the entry of the glamorous Meena with the famous actor–director–producer Kumar and, inevitably, they were surrounded by their fans and admirers. Compared to the young new favourites, these two had aged considerably, but they were still popular as a romantic team. The fans were noisy and boisterous, and Mahender had to use brute strength to extricate Meena and Kumar from their clutches. He had to manhandle a couple of them, but it could not be helped if the star pair was to be led to their seats. Then only could Mahender run inside for his imminent announcement. The show was about to begin. What was ringing shrilly now was the third, and final, bell.

2

The lights in the circus were gradually dimmed to complete darkness, and then the spotlight picked up the immaculate figure of Mahender. He was holding a microphone in his hand.

'Ladies and gentlemen,' he began to speak. But this was no routine announcement. His voice had a special, emotional quality, and he was carefully choosing his words to suit the occasion. 'Tonight is a memorable night in the history of our circus because, after many years, we are again privileged to present the performance of your beloved singing clown—Rajoo!'

Five thousand men, women and children in the packed galleries greeted the announcement with tumultuous applause. The three women and two men who were seated in the front row also joined in the clapping, but for them, it was not the start of a show, but the continuation of the story of their own life.

They all heard Mahender say—and each word had a poignant significance for them—'Where Rajoo disappeared all these years—what he did, what he gained and what he lost—he has not revealed even to me. But I do know this much—that wherever he was, whatever he was doing, whether he was happy or unhappy, well off or poor, healthy or sick, he was spreading laughter and happiness.'

Once again there was thunderous applause, but this time the three women forgot to applaud. Each of them was lost in her own thoughts, and in her own memories.

'Tonight Rajoo will perform again, he will sing again, he will laugh and make you laugh, the way you have never laughed in your life. Tonight is a memorable night for him, too.' Mahender cast a fleeting glance at the front-row seats reserved for Rajoo's personal guests—and noted that some of them were still unoccupied. 'Under the big top, in this very show, among you all, are present some of those whose love, sympathy and understanding, whose faith—*and whose faithlessness*—transformed an innocent boy into the greatest clown of the century.' And now Mahender directly faced the three women and two men seated in the front row, as if he were talking to them only. 'I do not know what they are thinking and feeling tonight but I want to tell them that whatever they have given to Rajoo was not wasted. The genius of the clown has assimilated it all, transformed it into the gift of laughter and generously distributed it to millions all over the world.'

Then the final announcement: 'Ladies and gentlemen, we give you the world's first, last and greatest singing clown—Rajoo.' And then, with a crash of music, there was sudden darkness.

3

When the lights came on, the circus ring was transformed into the operation theatre of some hospital. But this was unlike any other hospital. The doctors and nurses were all jokers. There were two big gas cylinders—one marked 'Hydrogen Bomb' and the other 'Nitrogen Bomb'. There was a huge bottle full of a red fluid, marked 'Blood'. There was a table loaded with giant-sized knives, forks, saws, hammers, chisels, forceps, and scissors.

Walking mechanically, comically, the chief surgeon entered with his assistant, both wearing surgeons' white smocks, and tall white caps like those worn by chefs. Shouting like the hectoring hero of the old-style theatre, the chief surgeon asked in a sing-song voice: 'What is the patient suffering from?'

The nurse replied, 'He suffers from an enlarged heart.'

'Very dangerous disease,' pronounced the surgeon. 'The world is small, the heart is big. We'll have to operate and take out the heart.' And then, like the announcer of a royal court, he shouted, 'Let the heart specialist come!'

The heart specialist and his assistant appeared, likewise dressed in surgeons' smocks and chefs' caps. The surgeon embraced the specialist, and both exchanged compliments. Elated, the heart specialist asked, 'What is he suffering from?'

'Too big a heart in too small a world!' informed the surgeon.

The heart specialist could hardly contain his joy. 'Then there is no hope. He can't survive.'

'What shall we do, then?'

'We must operate.'

'But will the operation save him?'

'Absolutely not.'

'Then why operate?' asked the assistant surgeon.

The assistant to the heart specialist loudly confided in his ear, 'The doctors will get their fees, whether the patient lives or dies. Let him die on the operation table.'

Another idea struck the chief surgeon. 'It's not merely the fees, but we'll have a chance to see a *big* heart. Otherwise, these days, whenever you open a man's chest, you take out a sparrow's heart!'

Then the anaesthetist was called. When he came,

wearing boxing gloves, the heart specialist asked, 'Doctor, what do you do?'

In reply, the anaesthetist hit his assistant who fell down, unconscious. 'That is what I do,' he declared proudly, 'knock down people unconscious.'

When all the other preparations were made, the doctors gathered around the operation table and removed the sheet covering the body. There was a gasp of surprise for there *was* no body!

'Where is the patient?'

'The patient has run away, fearing the surgeon's knife.'

'Then who will pay our fees, dammit?'

Meanwhile, one assistant doctor pointed upward. 'Look, there, an oversized heart is coming down from the heavens.'

Indeed, a very large heart was miraculously descending from the heavens—or from the big top of the circus. The doctors were watching it with curiosity, excitement, alarm.

The big heart—really a heart-shaped plastic drum—came down, then split open in the middle, and out came Rajoo. The Singing Clown! He doffed his hat and saluted the audience with an elaborate bow. The deafening applause lasted for several seconds. But the drama continued on the stage.

The surgeon went up to Rajoo the Joker. 'Are you a man or are you a heart?'

'The heart is the man, Doctor,' replied the Joker. 'There is a heart within a man, and a man—or woman—within a heart.'

One of the doctors informed the Joker, 'Do you know you are seriously ill?'

Another added, 'Get ready for the operation. We'll have to cut you up.'

On hearing this, Rajoo swooned and the doctors had to support him. Then he recovered his senses to ask, 'What am I suffering from, Doctor Saheb?'

'It is a frightful disease,' replied the surgeon. 'The world is shrinking, while your heart is getting bigger and bigger.'

'Then why don't you operate to stop the world from shrinking?' the Joker pleaded. 'Why do you want to take out *my* heart?'

But the doctors had to collect their fees and demonstrate their surgical skills. They pounced upon the poor Joker, laid him flat on the table; the anaesthetist placed the gas mask on his nose and released such a quantity of visible gas that soon the patient and the anaesthetist were knocked unconscious.

The surgeon and the heart specialist produced their hammers and their saws and, in a clown's parody of an operation, they cut up the Joker, they sawed through his ribs, they used hammers and tongs, they inserted huge forceps, they pulled and pulled, all together they puffed and they pulled, and only then did the forceps bring out a heart as big as a football.

No one had seen such a big heart.

The surgeon said, 'Such a big heart. The whole circus can be accommodated in this heart.' He handed over the heart to the specialist—in the process, the heart had become as big as a cushion.

The specialist said, 'Good god, it's become even bigger. Now it can encompass the whole city.'

Meanwhile, Rajoo had got up from the operation table and was going round the ring, searching for his heart, which was missing from his body. Again and again, he asked the spectators, 'Does any of you know who has stolen my heart?'

The audience roared with laughter.

But when he stood before the three women whom he had specially invited that night, there was no laughter when he asked, 'Have you stolen my heart?'

Mary, with the flicker of a sad smile, helplessly looked at her husband.

'Have you?' Rajoo's silent gesture asked Maria but her only answer was a sad sigh of resignation as she looked at the man whom she had helped to transform into a clown.

And now Rajoo, with his silent questioning look, was standing in front of the gorgeously dressed Meena, loaded with jewellery, who had a million rupees of black money in her locker. Under his scrutinizing look, she shivered, because she felt guilty, and naked, the poorest woman in the world because once she had traded her love for the tinsel of fame and fortune. She lowered her eyes in remorse and in shame.

Disappointed and disheartened, Rajoo returned to the group of doctors. 'Does anyone know who has stolen my heart?'

The surgeon, handing over the heart which was now bigger than a wrestler's broad chest, very seriously told Rajoo, 'Here is your heart. Keep it safe. If it continues to grow at this rate, a day will come when the whole world will walk into this heart.'

'Really, Doctor Saheb?' said Rajoo excitedly, holding the oversized heart in his hands. 'Will I be able to accommodate the whole world in my heart?' He was as overjoyed as if the doctor had given him news of winning a lottery.

And then a wave of music swept off everything—the hospital, the doctors, the nurses—and only the old Joker was left in the ring, playing about with his heart. He threw it here, he threw it there, he tossed it up, but every time the heart returned to him.

Once, he tossed it up very high and, as the heart was slowly coming down, for some reason, an involuntary and quickly muffled scream escaped the lips of the grey-haired Mary. Rajoo, startled, looked in her direction. In that split second, the heart hit the ground and, fragile as it was, broke into a hundred splintered pieces. The Joker stared at his broken heart, like a child who has smashed his own toy. He was fascinated by the broken pieces, for each of them reflected the image of Mary—not the grey-haired Mary but a younger Mary of thirty years ago. He felt himself swept by a wave of music that was carrying him back to the past, to the days of his adolescence.

Part One

TO MADAM, WITH LOVE

1

An unmusical sound, a peculiar grating, whirring sound, as if made by the fluttering wings of the Bird of Time, broke through the soft music.

As the veil of the past lifted, Rajoo found himself looking down at a snow-covered skating rink which seemed like a tank filled with milky white water in which many little fish were gliding.

Some were good skaters, and they whirled rapidly round the rink with great ease, and at great speed. Some were cautious and slowly took each measured step and sought the support of the ropes marking the boundary. Some of them were new and clumsy but reckless, and kept slipping and falling down with a thud. The clumsiest of them all was a fat boy in ill-fitting clothes, a thick home-knitted blue jersey that was too tight, and a woollen tasselled cap that was like the headgear of a clown. His face seemed familiar to Rajoo. Yes, now he knew. That boy was himself, Rajoo, at the age of fifteen. Once again he was the clumsy youth, feeling all the excitement and exhilaration of skating, of falling, of getting up again on faltering but venturesome legs.

And there she was—Mary, the best skater of all—a beautiful young woman of twenty-one or twenty-two, slim, taller than the boy Rajoo, in a form-fitting sweater of pink Angora wool that accentuated the disturbing, youthful curves of her breasts. She wore a fur cap, at a jaunty angle, over windblown soft black hair and had a half smile on her pink lips. She seemed to enjoy skating as she glided along, made circles, pirouetted, whirled on one leg, with the agility of an athlete and the grace of a dancer. Everyone watched her with envy and admiration.

For the boy Rajoo who had come for the first time to the skating rink (having saved his pocket money for a whole week to hire the skates for one hour!) it was difficult to skate and, at the same time, keep his eyes on the fascinating face and figure of the girl in the tight pink sweater. He ogled at her foolishly, with his mouth wide open, but every time he tried to propel himself on the skates to go near her, he fell down clumsily, amidst the laughter of the schoolboys. Rajoo did not mind the boys laughing at him and in fact joined them. He liked to laugh, even at his own discomfiture.

With the instinct of a showman, the boy found himself the centre of interest and attention, and repeatedly fell down with histrionic deliberation.

Now it was not a clumsy skater who was slipping and falling because of lack of balance, but a comedian or a clown who performed for the delight of the audience. But there was a method in his madness, and by his falling act, he hoped to attract the attention of the fairy like girl in pink.

Once, with great and careful effort, Rajoo managed to come skating near the girl, so near and so fast that he feared he might collide with her. He tried to stop, but of course he could not. He let himself fall down on the frozen snow, right at the feet of Mary. Once again, there was an outburst of laughter.

Mary turned round to see that a clumsy, fat, funny but good-looking boy had slipped and fallen and the rest of the boys and girls were laughing and jeering at him.

'Look there, that fatty has fallen again!'

'Fatty, are you searching for a rupee in the snow?'

'Eh, Fatso, if you don't know skating, why do you waste your money? Go home to your mother, Sonny Boy.'

Then they laughed aloud in chorus and, surprisingly enough, Rajoo joined in their laughter as he tried to get up and slipped once again.

Mary shouted at the boys with some authority in

her voice: 'Aren't you ashamed, laughing at a little boy because he has fallen down?'

Rajoo, still on the frozen ground, liked her interceding on his behalf but, somehow, did not like her referring to him as 'a little boy'.

When the boys, duly reprimanded, had sulked away, Mary extended her gloved hand to Rajoo who was still sprawled on the icy rink. 'Come, I will teach you how to skate—without falling.' Then she smiled a friendly, encouraging smile.

Rajoo gripped the proffered hand and got up on his feet. He didn't know why, but he liked the contact with that soft and warm hand, like a bird, within the leather glove.

Supporting and guiding him with her hands, she led him on to the centre of the rink and found that he skated without difficulty. He was enjoying himself in her company, but for the discomforting thought that she was taller, and older than him, and continued to talk to him as if to a little boy.

'You fell down so many times and everyone laughed at you,' she said sympathetically. 'Didn't you feel bad?'

'Why should I feel bad if people laugh?' he replied. 'It's better to fall down and make people laugh than to stand up and make people suffer and cry.'

'You sound like a little philosopher,' she remarked. 'What's your name?'

Rajoo raised his right hand in a characteristic gesture, and proclaimed, '*Mera naam*—Joker!'

'Joker?' she asked in surprise. 'What kind of a name is that?'

'Miss Saheb, my real name is Ranbir Raj. My mother calls me Rajoo. But in school, all the boys call me Joker. I stumble and fall to make people laugh, that's why!'

'School?' she said, slightly concerned. 'Which school do you attend?'

'Convent of Jesus.'

Raj had hardly uttered the words when Mary let go of his hand. 'Go on, you can now skate on your own,' she said and glided away, mixing with the crowd. She did not look back, even once.

Rajoo was left gaping at her receding form. He tried to catch up with her and in that attempt slipped, skidded, and sprawled on the ice, in a ridiculously comic position, accidental yet contrived.

2

The Convent of Jesus School had opened after the holidays. There was the usual noise and excitement of reunions, in and outside classrooms, in the corridors and in the quadrangles. The boys talked all at the same time, telling each other what they had done in the holidays, laughing and joking, with the boisterousness of their age.

In the eight standard classroom, the boys were discussing an important development.

'I hear we are getting a new class teacher.'

'Really? Who told you?'

'I get all the latest news from a clerk in the principal's office!'

'Let's wait and see what the new class teacher looks like!'

'I will show you what she looks like.' This was Rajoo who was standing by the empty teacher's chair, making a chalk drawing on the blackboard. When he finished, the boys saw that it was an old hag, stooped with age, and supporting herself on a stick. 'She's an old, grey-haired crone, toothless and doddering. She'll come and stammer, "Children, get up and stand on your heads!"'

The whole class roared with laughter. This Rajoo was a real clown, always thinking of new gags and pranks to make everyone laugh. They were still laughing when the class teacher appeared. The boys, suddenly silent and standing to attention, hoped she had not heard them. For this was no old hag, but a strikingly handsome young woman, wearing a white full-sleeved blouse, blue skirt, and high heels that came tapping over the tiled floor. Rajoo remained rooted to the spot near the blackboard, gaping foolishly and helplessly, for this was the very girl he had met the day before at the skating rink.

When she reached her table and chair, Mary saw the drawing on the blackboard and laughed good-humouredly. All the boys, except Rajoo, joined in the laughter.

'Do I look like this?' she asked the class.

'No, Madam,' came the boys' spontaneous reply in chorus. But Rajoo could not utter a word. Feeling guilty, embarrassed and nonplussed, he could only foolishly shake his head to say *no.*

'Sit down, boys,' said the teacher and, with a clattering of desks and scraping of feet, the boys took their seats. Rajoo was making his way to his desk in the rear when a boy suddenly extended his leg to trip him. Rajoo stumbled and fell flat on his face, causing laughter, and laughing at himself too.

When he was seated at last, and the hilarity had subsided, Mary too sat down to address her class. 'Children, our first meeting has auspiciously begun with laughter. I want you to be always happy, but it is easier to laugh at others. The great thing is to learn to laugh at yourself …'

'Is she referring to me?' Rajoo wondered. 'How friendly and kind she is! I feel I've known her for a long, long time.' His eyes were focused on her, and he listened intently to her every word. 'How sweet is her voice!' he thought.

Mary was now saying, 'Besides regular classes, I will also teach you drill, music and games. Don't regard me as only a teacher—I will also try to be your friend, your guide, your confidante whom you can trust and to whom you may bring your difficulties and problems. I am your friend, and you are mine!'

Rajoo felt that all this was said only for him, only to him. 'Yes, Teacher,' he told her but only in his thoughts, 'I'll regard you as my friend, my guide, my confidante—but what does it mean? Confidante? As soon as I reach home, I'll look up the dictionary!'

Now Mary was saying, 'To be mischievous is the birthright of all children. But only cowards tell lies. Whoever has made this cartoon, let him stand up!'

Rajoo briefly pondered over the moral dilemma. Should he tell the truth and face the consequences? It was not just the punishment of which he was afraid—she may ask him to stand up on the bench or even cane him—but what he was really worried about was that she might not be so kind and friendly towards him. Still, he decided to take the risk and stood up, his head bowed with shame.

The teacher recognized him at once, smiled, and then said, 'Well done, Rajoo!' He looked up, surprised, and heard her say, 'But your drawing is rather poor. I'll have to teach you drawing, too. Then you won't give such a stoop to my back.' The children laughed. 'Sit down,' she ordered Rajoo.

The teacher took a duster and rubbed the blackboard clean, then sat down and pulled out the attendance register.

'Purshottam Kumar.'

'Yes, Madam.'

'Anil Chanda.'

'Yes, Ma'am.'

'Qamruddin.'

'Yes, Ma'am.'

'Bunny Cooper.'

'Yes, Madam.'

'Gopal Varma.'

'Yes, Ma'am.'

While she was marking attendance, Rajoo stared fixedly at Mary. 'Of all the teachers,' he thought, 'why does she appeal to me most? Is it because she's a woman? But the last class teacher was also a woman.

Is it because she's young? But I've had other young teachers, too. But none had cast the same spell of fascination ... Why? Why?' Sorting out these puzzling thoughts, he didn't hear his name called out.

'Raj Ranbir!'

When she got no response, the teacher called the name again, and everyone in the class looked round at the absent-minded Rajoo who was obviously sleeping with his eyes wide open.

'Raj Ranbir! Rajoo!'

Rajoo woke up with a start and blurted out, 'Yes, Sir—No, Sir—No, Madam—I mean, Yes, Madam!'

While the class laughed, one of the boys explained, 'Madam, that's why we call him Joker!'

Everyone laughed again. Rajoo, too, burst out laughing. And he saw that the teacher, too, was chuckling. And the thought struck him, 'Is it only to me that the teacher looks ravishingly beautiful when she smiles?'

3

The boys in white shirts and shorts, in orderly formation on the school lawn, looked like a field of daffodils swaying in the breeze.

At least that's what Rajoo thought that morning. In particular, Mary, in a white half-sleeved shirt and divided skirt, reminded him of the daffodil that he had read about in a poem. 'Mary had a little lamb …' Another line of poetry came to his mind. Was he growing poetic, he wondered as he rhythmically moved his arms and legs along with all the boys. He had never enjoyed the drill period so much. Why?

Mary was demonstrating the Swedish exercises, and the boys were following her rhythmic movements.

She extended both her arms. All the boys extended their arms.

Mary raised her arms above her head. All the boys did the same.

Mary bent, keeping her knees straight, and touched her toes. All the boys bent and touched their toes …

All but one! When Rajoo bent down to touch his toes, there was a little tearing sound, like stitches giving way under strain. Rajoo got up and looked back, for the sound had come from behind him, and he thought some mischievous boy must be up to some tricks. But everyone was bending. So he decided there was nothing to worry about. When Mary bent again to touch her toes and all the boys followed her movement, Rajoo did the same—or tried to do the same. The moment he started bending, that little grating sound came again. Now he knew its origin. The seat of his half-pants was giving way—or had already given way—at the seams. He was in danger of being exposed. So he stood still, conspicuous among the hundred other boys who were exercising.

Mary noticed this and came towards him. 'Rajoo, why are you not doing the drill?'

'Madam,' he stuttered, keeping his left hand behind to cover the vital spot, 'it—is—rather—difficult.'

'Don't be silly,' Mary gently reprimanded him. 'It is not difficult at all. Do exactly as I do. Like this. One. Inhale. Two. Exhale. Three. Bend down. Keep the knees straight. Touch your toes. Four. Get up.'

But Rajoo couldn't do this, he kept standing, feeling embarrassed, and then he had to blurt out, 'Madam, I am sorry, I can't do it—because the seat of my shorts is torn.'

He had not spoken aloud, but the few children who heard him guffawed, and one of them said, 'Fatty, why do you eat so much? You are bursting at the seams, all over!'

'Silence!' ordered Mary. Then she blew the whistle to disperse the boys. To Rajoo she said, 'Come with me.'

Rajoo was a day scholar, so he had not seen it, but as in every other boarding school, their convent, too, had a linen room where, along with sheets, towels, pillowcases, mattresses and curtains, there was a pedal sewing machine and other accessories for emergency tailoring. There were white-painted partitions for the school hospital too.

Behind one such partition stood Rajoo, feeling shy and embarrassed, only keeping his head above the curtains. Threading a needle, Mary said, 'Come on, Rajoo, give me your shorts.'

Rajoo flushed visibly and stammered, 'But, Madam—I—I mean—how can I? I feel shy, Madam, to take them off.'

Mary laughed but not unkindly. 'It is for the girls to feel shy. Are you a girl?'

Rajoo felt even more acutely embarrassed but, finding no answer, he took off the shorts behind the curtain and gingerly handed them over the partition.

Mary saw that only the stitching had given way at the back, the fabric was intact. Placing it on the sewing machine, while working the pedal, she said, 'Don't worry, I will make it secure in no time.' Then, just to keep the conversation going, she asked, 'Where did you get it stitched?'

Rajoo reluctantly admitted, 'Madam, you see my

mother sewed it in a hurry, so maybe the stitching was not strong enough.'

'Your mother can do tailoring, too?' Mary asked, duly impressed.

'Yes, Madam, she stitches all my clothes. The tailors are so expensive, and she can't afford them. We are poor, you know!'

'Never say such a thing,' Mary warned him affectionately. 'Who says you are poor? You never tell lies, you are honest and upright, intelligent and yet modest. You have all the riches of good character and conduct. Who can call you poor?' Then, handing over the repaired shorts to Rajoo, she asked, 'What's the name of your mother?'

'I know her only as Ma!'

'And what does your father do?'

'He is no more—he is dead!'

'Oh, I am sorry. But what did he do, while he was alive?'

'When he died, I was just a year old. Beyond that, my mother doesn't tell me anything.'

Mary was surprised. 'Doesn't tell you anything about your father?' Then she chose not to pursue the questioning, but already her curiosity had caused a smouldering disturbance in the mind of the fifteen-year-old Rajoo.

After school, when Rajoo reached home, he saw that his mother, a widow with the telltale marks of hard work and exhaustion on her once-beautiful features, was busy with the sewing machine. Seeing her only son, she beamed with a mother's joy. 'Come, Rajoo. Try this shirt I have just stitched for you.'

But Rajoo was in a belligerent mood. 'I don't want a new shirt,' he shouted, though only last week he had specifically asked for it.

'What, what has happened to you?' The mother was taken aback by her son's truculence.

At last Rajoo blurted out the question that was gnawing at his brain. 'Ma, tell me first, what was my father's profession?'

This was the one question that Rajoo's mother always avoided answering though, in her heart, she knew that one day she will have to reveal everything. She tried to evade it again. 'Arrey, you are tired after all that learning in school. Wash your face and I will give you something to eat.'

But Rajoo was not to be so easily taken in. 'No, I won't eat, now or ever, unless you tell me what my father did for a living. In school, every boy is proud of his father and his father's profession. Bunny Cooper's daddy is a doctor, Gopal's father is a mill owner, Anwar's father is a barrister. Today the new teacher asked me what my father did and I could not answer her. You say that he is dead. But what did he do before died? Why don't you tell me? Was he something for me to be ashamed of—a pauper, a criminal, a murderer?'

'Stop it!' For once, his mother shouted. 'I will tell you what your father did for a living!'

She went quickly to the inner room, rummaged a drawer, took out something, and then threw it at her son, saying, 'This was your father!' There were tears in her eyes and her voice was choked.

Rajoo looked down and saw a doll dressed as a clown. The little joker was staring up at him with his lifeless blue glass eyes. Slowly, the boy picked up the doll, looked at it; deeply stirred, his face wrinkled into a smile.

'So, my father, too, was a joker!' He said it proudly, as if he had been a governor, or a minister, or a big government officer. 'Did he really live to make people laugh?'

At last, she had revealed the awful secret that she had kept hidden in her heart all these years. Tears were flowing from her eyes as she spoke.

'Yes, he lived to make people laugh. They used to say there never was a clown like him. Every night he went to the circus, the spectators laughed and laughed till they could laugh no more. The circus was his whole existence. He always sang the refrain—"*Jeena yahaan, marna yahaan, iske siwa jaana kahaan?*" And he died in the circus, and till the end he made people laugh. When he fell from the trapeze, and there was an accident, the spectators mistook it for a new gag and, as he lay dying, people roared with laughter ...'

There were tears in the mother's eyes and a new light, a new resolve, in the eyes of her son. 'Ma, when I grow up, I will also become a clown. I, too, will live to make people laugh.'

The mother reacted as if a sudden fit of madness had seized her. 'So you, too, will become a clown?' And, saying this, she gave a resounding slap to her son who was so shocked that he forgot even to cry or to protest. The old woman was now hysterically crying, 'One killed himself to make people laugh, leaving a widow and an orphan to weep over him. And now you say you'll also become a joker, a clown. Why do you think I'm slaving night and day to give you the best education in such an expensive school? Is it to make you a circus clown so that you, too, should die one day, while making people laugh? Speak up, will you become a clown? Will you, too, desert your mother like your father did? Speak up, you fool.' She rained a series of hysterical blows on Rajoo's cheeks.

But then she embraced him, and kissed him, and tearfully pleaded with him. 'My son, my darling, I want you to study hard, to get a good job, become a great man, and then to bring home a fairy like daughter-in-law, so that at last I should know some peace, some happiness, in the last years of my life.'

The mother continued to cry, hugging the son to her bosom but, behind the mother's back, the son was smiling affectionately, longingly, at the little joker, as if it were the soul of his father that was inviting him to share his destiny!

4

In the music class, Mary had just asked the children what instruments they could play.

One said, 'I can play the harmonium.'

A fat boy, in a booming voice, said, 'I can play the drum.'

A thin boy piped in with, 'A flute, Madam.'

And a boy, who was neither thin nor fat, very seriously announced, 'I can play the gramophone, Madam,' which sent the whole class into peals of laughter.

The laughter faded out when they heard a tune being played on the mouth organ. There was something beautiful but melancholic about that tune. Even Mary turned to the door just as Rajoo entered, hiding behind him the little musical instrument.

'Were you playing on the mouth organ?' she asked.

Guiltily, Rajoo confessed, 'Yes, Madam.'

'Then play it again. Let's hear it!'

Rajoo brought out the mouth organ, pressed it to his lips and blew into it. Tilting his head and closing his eyes, he began to play. As he played, even the most boisterous boys were silenced. There was something in the tune, something sad, and hauntingly lilting, that cast a spell on everyone.

When Rajoo had played a few bars and stopped, Mary said, 'You play it very well. Let's hear some other tune.'

'No, Madam, I can't play any other tune. This is the only one I know.'

'Would you like me to teach you another tune?' she asked, and Rajoo wanted to say *yes*, but he shook his head. 'No, Madam.'

'Why?'

'For me, one melody is enough for one life.'

Mary thought this boy was quite a philosopher. Then she asked, 'Are there any words to this tune?'

'There is a song that my father used to sing. I know

only the refrain—"*Jeena yahaan, marna yahaan, iske siwa jaana kahaan?*"'

Mary was surprised and saddened to hear a child uttering such sombre words. 'Who had taught him this song?' she thought. His father? Who was he? What was he? Did the boy understand the fatalistic message implicit in this refrain? But, aloud, she said, 'Rajoo, this is a beautiful tune, but the song is too pessimistic for a young man like you who is standing on the threshold of his life. I will teach you a new song.'

Rajoo looked at his teacher and found a smile hovering over her lips. 'First, she taught me skating,' he thought, 'then she taught me self-respect. Now she's going to teach me a new tune, a new song. It seems I have a lot to learn from this kind teacher, not merely history, geography and English composition and other subjects in the syllabus!'

From within his heart he sensed a new music, a new rhythm of life set to new hopes, desires and ambitions, but also to a new and undefinable pain. And he thought to himself: 'What is happening to me? What has happened to me?'

5

Rajoo would never forget the day Mary took the boys of his class on a weekend picnic, for it was the last day of his childhood. The whole day they sang and played their various musical instruments, tried to catch partridges (though, with all their elaborate nets, they were unable to catch a single bird), cooked their own food, and sat to an alfresco lunch. Mary was good company. She laughed with them and she sang with them, she taught them new and funny songs, and the lines she sang, they all repeated in chorus. Rajoo enjoyed every minute of it, accompanying her songs on his harmonica. 'How well Madam sings,' he thought, 'but I, too, am no less an artiste—no one can play the harmonica like me!' Perhaps that was the ideal relationship between teacher and student—a sense of belonging to each other. Let not the boys be afraid of their teacher. Here was a friend, indeed! What had she said that day? 'I am your friend, your guide, your confidante.' What does confidante mean? He sure didn't know, for he'd forgotten to consult the dictionary. He made a mental note to look up its meaning as soon as he reached home.

By the evening, most of the boys were to be found plunging into a river that was not too wide or too deep. The swimmers swam about, teaching the beginners how to keep themselves afloat. Others were content to stand in knee-deep water, hitting the water to splash each other. But Rajoo was scared of getting into the river. He had never even ventured into the school swimming pool. (The additional fee was five rupees a month!) So he sat on the grassy bank, watching the others swimming or splashing about. There were colourful sunset clouds in the sky—just like the ones in the big painting in the school library. As the sun was going down, the evening breeze had a pleasant edge to it. Rajoo contemplated, with envy, the hardy and brave boys who were swimming, or diving, or wading, or just splashing in the river!

Rajoo had an inkling of what they were up to when Farooq shouted, 'Come on, Rajoo, come down into the water, man!'

Rajoo shook his head apologetically. 'No, yaar. I don't know how to swim.'

Gopal slowly advanced through the water, saying, 'He won't agree so easily. Let's drag him into the river!'

Two boys came forward to grab Rajoo who started whimpering, 'No, no, yaar. I feel very cold!'

Farooq caught Rajoo's legs and said to the others,

with a mischievous glint in his eyes, 'Let's take off his pant and throw him in the water.'

'No, no, please!' Rajoo was now pleading, while two boys clung to his legs, and the third was pulling down his pant. 'I feel very very cold and the river is all wet, I tell you, just like water!' He was blurting out whatever came to his mind and whatever, in his opinion, would secure his release. 'Listen to me, friends. It's very serious. No joking matter, I tell you. If you drag me into the water, I will catch malaria—I mean, pneumonia. Double pneumonia.'

Then, as the boys were about to pull off his pant, he shouted, 'Help! Help! They are drowning me!'

The shouts were loud enough to be heard by Mary who was relaxing at a distance in the shade of a tree, reading a book. She thought someone was drowning and started running frantically along the river's edge.

She was shouting questions even as she was running. 'Who is it? Who is drowning? Speak up, boys, speak up ...'

The moment the boys saw the teacher running towards them, they jumped into the river or slunk out of view. Others pretended to look the other way, innocently unconcerned.

Rajoo, at last freed from the clutches of his tormentors, and buttoning his trousers, was no less unnerved than the others, as he saw the teacher coming in his direction.

Mary still did not know what had caused the commotion. 'What happened?' she repeatedly asked. 'Is someone drowning?'

At last Farooq volunteered the information. 'No, Madam. But these boys were trying to drown Rajoo because he wouldn't get into the water!'

Mary, alarmed, looked at Rajoo and when she was reassured that he was safe, she let the boys have it: 'How many times have I warned you not to play the fool, not to drag into the river someone who doesn't know swimming!' She was now walking along the slippery, moss-covered edge of the riverbank. 'But you boys are incorrigible. You don't realize how it can ...' She could not complete her sentence, for just then her sandalled feet slipped over the muddy slope, and the next moment she fell into the river. The boys couldn't resist laughing.

Where she fell, the river was not deep at all. Mary recovered her balance soon enough, and now Rajoo's eyes saw the vision of a sea nymph (more beautiful than the one in their school book!) emerging from the water. The thin silk frock, dripping with water, was clinging to her body, and was now wrinkled up on one side, revealing the smooth alabaster legs up to her thighs. He furtively looked at the curves of her breasts, accentuated by the thin, wet fabric, and was dismayed and disturbed by what he saw. He lowered his eyes, and now he could see only a pair of trim ankles and shapely feet shining with drops of water.

The laughter of the boys provoked the teacher to deliver a further reprimand. 'Learn some manners, all of you. You are not uncouth loafers from the streets. Now, get out. Enough of swimming. Go and change into dry clothes. Come on, hurry up.'

The boys meekly obeyed, their dripping bodies, one after another, coming out of the water. Their sidelong glances made Mary self-conscious about her wet clothes and she quickly walked away towards a cluster of trees and bushes, not far from the river.

Rajoo could have solemnly sworn that he had not deliberately planned to pursue his teacher. Since catching a glimpse of the sea nymph rising out of the water, he was experiencing a strange restlessness. He did not feel like talking to anyone. He wanted to be alone, and so he drifted away from the chattering, gossiping clusters of boys.

He was aimlessly walking along the riverbank, when he was warned by some sort of movement in the distant bushes. Could it be a wild animal, even a tiger? They had heard that the striped cats roamed the nearby jungles. In sheer panic, he was rooted to the spot, thinking which way to run. But then he saw that it was not an animal, but a human being with feet and bare legs, glimpsed between the bushes. Man or woman? A man's legs can't be so fair and so smooth. It must be a woman. The disturbing thought flashed through his mind—it must be Madam! Their teacher. Why is she hiding in the bushes? Then he knew she must be wringing and drying her wet clothes. But then she must be … His heart beat faster with a pleasurable sense of guilt. He took a few steps forward and then taking cover behind a tree, peeped cautiously in the direction of the bushes, straining his eyes to view the forbidden mystery. He saw just a fleeting glimpse—the stems of two long, smooth legs, partly seen through the bushes, then the overhanging branches covering part of the torso, a slim waist, and then two full breasts struggling within the narrow confines of a pink brassiere. The face above was familiar, but it looked even more fascinating at this moment, framed as it was by dark, wet tresses from which drops of water were dripping on her rose-petal cheeks.

He had a glimpse, just one glimpse, and he was unnerved. No one had seen him. Madam was completely oblivious to any prying eyes. Her privacy secured by the green leafy screen, she was unselfconsciously wringing her wet clothes and spreading them on the grass to dry. But Rajoo's own conscience was stricken with a sense of guilt. He ran from there in panic, a hundred demons pursuing him.

He ran, racing through the cluster of trees, across the ploughed fields, along the riverbank, and the whole jungle seemed to be running after him, the trees going round and round, the river water gurgling obscenities, demons were at his heels.

Rajoo had an uncanny feeling that he was not only running *away* from some frightening spectre, he was also running towards someone. Was it his carefree childhood, the age of innocence, that was at that moment running away from him? He tried to catch up with it, to restrain it, to persuade it to stay. But once frightened out of its innocence, childhood scampers away and never returns. When it goes, it goes forever!

Every night, tired after the day at school, Rajoo's head had no sooner touched his pillow than he was fast asleep. But, that night, for the first time, Rajoo could not sleep. He kept awake, restlessly tossing and turning in his bed. Even when he tightly closed his eyes to count sheep, he was haunted by that pink spectre, that disturbingly beautiful face, those slender legs, those mysterious curves of the breasts, those cherry-red lips. 'Why should the glimpse of a human body so disturb me?' he thought. 'Why can't I sleep tonight? Why? Why?' He was tortured by questions, by doubt, by an inexplicable pain, by a mysterious pleasure. And by a sense of guilt. He had vague fears that to even think about such mysteries was a sin.

That face and that body belonged to his teacher.

It was the face of the one he called 'Madam'. Madam! Madam! Madam!

From the depths of his heart rose a secret yearning. If only she was not his teacher, if only she was not older than him!

If only she had been just Mary!

Mary—Mother of God! No, no. The convent-educated boy hastily made a sign of the cross as atonement for what he thought were blasphemous thoughts.

No, not Mary, Mother of God.

Mary.

Just Mary!

Whose Mary?

Mine!

Then at last he drifted into sleep. But his dreams were as daring, as disturbing as his reckless thoughts!

6

The next day, as he sat in the classroom, Rajoo could not, for the life of him, concentrate on what Madam was teaching. He felt feverish, his face was flushed with the onrush of blood, and he felt choked. He opened his collar button, loosened the old school tie, but he still felt choked.

I have sinned! I have sinned! This thought, this fear, this accusation, kept hammering in his brain. I have sinned! I have sinned!

He remembered the day when, at the end of school, he was passing through the chapel and saw Madam Mary, devoutly kneeling before the statue of Christ.

He, too, was fascinated by the idea, and had decided to do the same.

When Mary finished her prayers, and made a sign of the cross, she turned and was surprised to find Rajoo, a Hindu, kneeling like a devout Catholic.

'Rajoo, what are *you* doing here?'

'You were kneeling, so I thought I'll do the same.' And he had innocently asked, 'Why do you do it?'

'To beg forgiveness for our wrongdoings. The love of Christ washes away all our sins.'

Then, looking intently at the image of the Saviour, Rajoo asked: 'Madam, in every picture, in every statue, Christ is always sad. I've never seen Christ laughing or even smiling. Why is He so sad?'

'Because His children, the people of the world, are afflicted with so many sorrows.'

'Does He become sad because I am sad?'

'Yes. He loves you. So, if you are sad He must be sad, too.'

'Then I'll never be sad. And one day I'll make Him laugh!' Was he imagining or was there the merest flicker of a smile on the face of Christ?

As he remembered that incident, it occurred to Rajoo that there might be atonement for his sin if he prayed before the image of Christ. But how could he go out of the class?

The teacher was dictating homework for the holidays, and all the boys were diligently writing in their notebooks. As Mary casually looked in his direction, she saw that Rajoo was not writing. He seemed to be dreaming with his eyes open. She walked up to him. 'Rajoo, you are not writing your homework?'

'No, Madam—er, Madam ...' He was confused and flustered as he pulled out a textbook out of his desk.

Mary asked in surprise, 'Will you write the homework in this book?' Then, sensing there was something wrong with him, she asked, 'What's the matter, Rajoo? Are you ill?'

Rajoo said, 'Yes, Madam, I don't feel well.'

'Why didn't you say so before? Let me see if you have fever.' As Mary extended her hand to touch his forehead, Rajoo pulled back his head in time. He was afraid that if Madam's soft and delicate hand touched him, he would like it, and that, too, would be a sin.

'No, Madam, there's no fever—it's nothing, really,' he said confusedly, 'only I don't feel well.'

Mary was a little worried by the boy's confused state. 'Whatever it is, you get up. Go home and rest. Come on, get up.'

Rajoo got up, collected his books and slowly walked out of the classroom. Mary watched him go, and wondered what had suddenly happened to the lively and mischievous Rajoo. 'Maybe,' she thought, 'the poor boy has some problems at home.'

After school, when Mary as usual entered the chapel, she was a little more than surprised to find Rajoo kneeling before the altar. He was muttering some prayers, which were inaudible at a distance.

'Sir, Sir,' Rajoo was muttering under his breath, 'I have committed a sin, a great sin. They say if we confess before you, all sins are washed away by your love. Sir, I pull my ears, I promise you I will not do such a sinful thing again—please forgive me, Sir.'

He saw that there was great kindness and compassion on the gentle face of Christ, and he felt that Christ had forgiven him.

'Thank you, Sir,' he said, a little louder, as he got up. 'Thank you, indeed, Sir!'

Now Mary came forward. 'Rajoo, what on earth are you doing here? Why haven't you gone home?'

Rajoo could not face Mary. He kept his eyes lowered as he said, 'Madam, I was praying for forgiveness for my sins.'

'Sins?' she repeated, in disbelief. 'Children don't commit any sins. You are only a child ...'

Rajoo felt insulted, humiliated. Now he looked up at Mary, then looked back at Christ. Then, looking at Mary, he said, 'Madam, I am no longer a child.' Then he quickly walked out of the chapel.

Now only Mary was left there—and the image of Jesus Christ. A thoughtful and puzzled Mary.

But, on the stone face of Christ, there was a serene smile of compassion for those of His children who are in a hurry to discard their innocence—and yet cannot!

7

Schoolboys all over the world, and especially in boarding schools, eagerly look forward to the annual vacations. Now they would be free from classes, physical training drill, hostel food, and the code of discipline. They would be able to meet their parents and brothers and sisters, eat all their favourite delicacies especially prepared by Mother, see as many cinema shows as they can, and, most important of all, sleep when they like and get up from bed at any late hour.

All the boys of the Convent of Jesus School were excited about the beginning of the holidays. There was jubilation everywhere; trunks, suitcases, holdalls and bedding rolls were being packed, addresses were being exchanged, and plans for the holidays were being made and discussed. Since the school was situated in the hills, there was only one small-gauge train that came and went to the junction station in the plains. For the day, the whole train was reserved by the school authorities, and now the platform was overcrowded with boys in school blazers. Mary, who was accompanying the children, was in charge of all the arrangements, and so all the questions were being addressed to her.

'Madam, which is our compartment?'

'Madam, where shall we sit?'

'Madam, can we put our luggage here?'

'Madam, these boys aren't letting us enter the compartment.'

Even in the midst of all the rush and confusion, Mary was smilingly tackling the situation. 'You sit here.' 'You go to that compartment.' 'You keep your luggage in compartment number four.' She was surrounded by excited boys of all shapes and sizes, bubbling with eagerness to get on the train. But her eyes were searching for a boy who was not going by this train, who was not going anywhere.

He was, at the time, taking out that little clown doll from the cupboard, remembering all his mother had said about the poverty and privations they had had to endure. 'You are like me—nowhere to go in the holidays.'

Rajoo had asked his mother: 'Ma, why don't we go somewhere during the holidays? All the boys go somewhere or the other, have lots of fun, only I remain here, all alone.'

The mother had replied, 'Son, how can we afford it? You know with what difficulty I manage to pay for your school. When the holidays come, I have to work extra hard to collect money for the next term fees. Study well, pass your exams, and try to become a man of consequence. Then there will be time enough to roam around the country and even around the world.'

But Rajoo never wanted to become a man of consequence. He was going to be neither a leader nor a lawyer nor a doctor nor an administrator—he wanted to be only a joker. Like the little clown-doll who was the symbol of his father!

From a distance came the warning whistle blast of the railway engine. It reminded Rajoo that his friends were going by that train. And Mary! A good teacher, after all, was a good friend, too!

Running over the hilly slopes, Rajoo took a shortcut to the station just as the train was about to start. On the crowded platform, several of his friends tried to engage him in conversation, but Rajoo had no time for them. With a brief 'Ta-ta, bye-bye', he took leave of them and made his way to where Mary was giving last-minute instructions to the boys who now clambered up the footboards.

'Rajoo!' Mary shouted to him as she saw him running towards her, panting and puffing. Poor fellow, he must have come from a long distance.

'Yes, Madam,' he said, quite breathless by the time he reached her, 'I—I came to—see you—all—off!'

'Thank you, Rajoo,' said Mary, and noticed something wrapped up in a paper which he was holding behind him. 'What is that you are hiding?'

Rajoo promptly handed over the packet to Mary, but his nervousness was apparent. 'It's for you, Madam.'

Mary opened the packet and was surprised to find inside the little joker. Why was a doll being presented to her?

'What's this?'

'This is the joker,' replied Rajoo, and then, summoning all his courage, he blurted out, 'It's me!'

In all the noise and the crowd and the excitement of departure, Mary could not understand the underlying significance of that remark. She only saw what was apparent, that a mischievous boy of her class had chosen a funny present for her. Holding up the little joker, she said, 'Very sweet and very naughty—just like you!'

The train siren sounded for the last time, the guard blew his whistle, and waved the green flag, the boys leaned out of the windows to sing the school song in chorus. Mary, too, climbed the footboard, just as the train started moving, but she stood in the open door of her compartment, holding up the little joker to say goodbye to Rajoo who was running alongside the train, waving his hand.

Then the train passed out of the platform, and Rajoo was left standing there, still waving goodbye. The train was taking Mary away and soon disappeared in a tunnel, leaving behind a cloud of black smoke. Rajoo suddenly felt a great emptiness within him, but he was consoled by the thought that he had been able to present the little joker to Madam, and that she had accepted it and taken it with her.

8

Rajoo had read somewhere, in his poetry book, the expression 'Bird of Time', and Mary had explained that time was always fleeting, that it never stopped, and so it was likened to a bird that had wings, and was constantly flying away.

But now Rajoo realized that the poet was wrong. Madam was wrong. Time was not a bird at all. Time was a snail and moved incredibly slowly.

These were the longest vacations Rajoo ever had. It seemed they would never end. Life had become empty, dull, monotonous. It had become a burden. Rajoo felt listless and sluggish, he had no interest in anything. Early in the morning, his mother left for her job in the sanatorium where she worked as a matron. Then Rajoo would feel suffocated in the little house. He went out in the cold, and here, too, only desolation met his eye. The autumn leaves were scattered everywhere, and they crackled under his feet. The trees were leafless, bare, and seemed to be shivering in the cold breeze. There was no greenery anywhere, no flowers, no colour, no life. A perpetual fog enveloped the town. Even the little bazaar was practically deserted, the few passersby, muffled in overcoats or blankets or shawls, walked swiftly, silently, like ghosts.

Their school, too, was deserted and desolate. The quadrangles, the classrooms, the library, the playing fields which were always filled with the sounds of life and laughter—over everything lay now the shroud of eerie silence. Rajoo walked through the empty corridors, like a lost soul, and heard the echoes of his own footsteps. The emptiness was frightening. Yet it held a peculiar fascination, for the next day he would go there again to savour the silence and the emptiness that matched the desolation in his own heart!

In all this isolation, he never thought of seeking diversion in the few places that drew crowds during the severest cold wave—the station, the tea shops, the cinema. He was now used to walking alone. People would see Rajoo walking through the streets, his hands deep in his pockets, his collar turned up against the biting cold, muttering to himself. For, despite his loneliness, Rajoo was not alone. There was his friend and constant companion—the joker within him—with whom he carried on long and animated, but silent, conversation—or, rather, catechism.

'Who are you?'

'I am the joker.'

'Then, who am I?'

'You are also the joker.'

'What is life?'

'It is freezing cold, the season of autumn, poverty, loneliness. And death!'

'What is death?'

'Death is a witch who carried away my father. One day it will carry away Mother—and then it will carry away me, too!'

'What is the safest, softest, warmest refuge in the world?'

'It's my mother's lap, where I feel most safe and secure.'

'What is the most beautiful being in the world?'

'That is Madam. That is Mary. When she smiles, it is like the sun coming out on a cold, foggy winter day;

when she laughs, it is like the music of the mountain stream; who is beautiful in reality, and even more beautiful in dreams; who is my teacher but more than a teacher; who is my friend but more than a friend; who is softness and warmth, but different from the softness and warmth I get in my mother's lap.'

'Then what is she?'

'She is life and laughter, flowers blooming in springtime, she is the softness of silk, and the mellow sweetness of honey. Her name is Mary and she is mine. But I won't reveal this fact to anyone, or people will snatch her away from me. She will continue to live in my thoughts, I will keep her safely locked in my heart. She, her beauty and sweetness and warmth, will become a part of my being, and no one will know—not even she.'

'Well, friend, is this the feeling called love?'

'This question even I have not dared to ask myself. Who are you to ask me?'

'Who am I?' The friend within chuckled. 'I am the joker who lives within you.'

9

From a distance came the welcome sound of a train whistle, and Rajoo suddenly realized that the holidays were over, today everyone would be coming back—everyone including Mary!

As he ran out of the house, he saw that the grim Winter was vanquished by the armies of Spring. Everything was now covered with green. Spring flowers were blooming everywhere. Quickly, he plucked an armful of wild flowers, and then he ran to the station. The path ran along the railway line, and he reached in time to see the train coming in, decorated with red and blue and yellow and green banners; the boys looking out of the windows were singing the school song, the school band playing to the rhythm of the train wheels. Rajoo was so happy that, as he ran alongside the train, he started handing over the flowers to his friends who were leaning out of the windows.

By the time the train stopped on the platform, Rajoo's armful of flowers had been reduced to a small bunch which he had saved for Mary. There she was, coming down from the train, looking radiantly happy and beautiful. Rajoo greeted her with his bouquet of wild flowers.

'Hello, Rajoo,' she said, accepting the flowers. 'Thanks!'

Still breathless and panting after his cross-country run, and too excited to speak, Rajoo took off his cap and brought out a red rose which, too, he proceeded to present to her.

'Oh, thank you again. How did you enjoy the holidays?'

'They were too long, Madam. Didn't seem to end.'

'That's surprising,' said Mary. 'Most of the boys complain the vacation is not long enough. Why didn't you enjoy your holidays?'

Rajoo simply told her the truth. 'Because you were not here. The whole school lay deserted.'

Mary was still pondering the significance of the remark when a young man, tall and well-built, wearing a tweed coat and slacks, got down from the compartment. The way he took down the suitcases, he seemed to be on informal and intimate terms with Mary.

'I wish he turns out to be Madam's brother!' prayed Rajoo secretly.

'David!' Mary addressed the tall young man with complete informality. 'Meet Rajoo—the brightest boy in my class.' And, then turning to Rajoo, she said, 'This is David.'

David took Rajoo's hand in his iron grip and said, 'How do you do? What name did you say, young man?'

Rajoo raised his right arm and proclaimed, '*Mera naam* Joker!'

'Joker?' replied David, somewhat surprised, and then thinking it was some kind of schoolboy joke, he laughed good-heartedly.

David was about to pick up the suitcases when Rajoo offered his services. 'Leave these to me, Sir.'

The boys had all got into the buses when David and Mary, arm in arm, came out of the station, Mary marching in step with David's long strides. Far behind them, walking slowly, dragged down by the weight of the suitcases, and terribly depressed, came Rajoo. He gloomily noted that the sun that was shining so hopefully a few minutes ago was now covered with dark clouds, and that a cold wind was blowing.

10

The holidays over, the school routine resumed. Mary took Rajoo's classes, supervised their physical training, gave them music lessons. But for Rajoo, it was the same sense of loneliness and desolation as when she was not there during the long vacation. When she took attendance and called out 'Raj Ranbir', and he responded with 'Yes, Madam', she marked him present even without raising her eyes to confirm his presence. As soon as the classes were over, she was always in a hurry to go back home to her rooms in the staff quarters. She seldom even paused in the chapel.

Why had Madam changed? Why didn't she take the same interest in her work? The boys often discussed the likely reasons for this, but whenever the topic was talked about, Rajoo avoided the gossiping circle. He knew the scandal-mongering that went on behind her back. He disliked anyone gossiping about Madam. Sometimes, when he overheard it, he would even have violent arguments. 'Eh, shut up. Don't you dare say dirty things about our madam.' But boys will be boys, and tongues continued to wag all over the campus. Actually, whispered gossip had begun on the very day the boys came back after the holidays. Rajoo remembered how he had carried Mary's and David's suitcases to the taxi they had hired to take them, and not even once had they suggested that they would give a lift to Rajoo and drop him on the way!

Smarting from this rebuff, he got into one of the school buses. Sunder had called him and said, 'Come on, sit here. I will tell you something very, very interesting.'

When Rajoo took his seat and the bus had started, Sunder said, 'Rajoo, what a romantic drama we saw in the train! Madam and David were in the same compartment. They were holding hands …' He demonstrated it by taking Rajoo's hand in his and squeezing it. '… Like this!'

Govind had volunteered further details. 'And, Rajoo, I must tell you this. Madam was peeling the apple and cutting it into slices and feeding David like a baby. It's a regular love affair. Mark my words: Wedding bells will ring soon for David and Madam. It's a real Romeo–Juliet drama, I tell you!'

Rajoo had suddenly and unaccountably flared up. He had shouted at Govind, 'Don't spread dirty scandal about Madam. She can never do such things!' And then he had called out to the bus driver. 'Stop. Stop the bus. I have to get down here.' He had got down at least a mile away from his house, and had to walk along the lonely, dimly lit road, thinking all the time that these boys had dirty minds. 'Who knows David may be Madam's brother, or cousin, or an old family friend. Why should they make a scandal about a simple friendship?' And yet, he also knew that, while he would not talk like the others, he too did not relish David's intimacy with Madam!

That was some weeks ago. Since then the gossip about Madam and David had gained ground and was discussed quite openly. Everyone kept track of the developments, and when these were lacking, they invented theories and surmises. One would say they were getting married soon. Another held that they had married during the holidays but, for some reason, they were not publicly announcing it. Some swore that they had seen them kissing each other in the garden. And some said—but the boys talked of things that were unrepeatable, even in one's thoughts!

One day it was raining. They had a free period, or Mary had taken leave and not come to school. 'It's raining so hard,' Rajoo thought. 'Maybe Madam has fallen ill. I must go and see her. But what will I say when she asks why I've come?'

Luckily for him, when he went into the library, the librarian said, 'Rajoo, do you know why your Madam has stopped coming to the library? Two weeks ago she had ordered some books, but since then she has had no time to look in.'

Rajoo had a brainwave. 'Give me the books. Her house is on my way. I'll deliver them.'

The librarian welcomed the idea and handed over the two volumes, but warned Rajoo. 'Be careful of the rain.'

Rajoo reassured him, 'Don't worry. I've got an umbrella.'

Rajoo's umbrella had inspired many jokes and legends. Everyone made fun of it, and the owner did not mind it. It was said, for instance, that it rained as much *under* Rajoo's umbrella as over it. Holding the broken, battered and hole-ridden umbrella over his head, and carrying the precious two volumes under his jacket for extra protection, Rajoo splashed his way to Mary's bungalow, and wished he hadn't gone.

There was a heavy downpour, and the bungalow was only dimly visible through the curtain of rain. But one of the doors was open, and the lights were on. He saw a two-headed silhouette and, as he went nearer, the silhouette split into two figures. One man and one woman who were very near each other, so near that (Rajoo thought) they must be suffocating each other. David and Madam. Madam and David!

Rajoo hesitated to enter, thought of running away from there, but he had already been observed. David, who was facing the door, saw him first and said, 'Mary, look, there's your student—Rajoo!'

'Come in, Rajoo, come in,' Mary called out, adding in a whisper aside to David, 'poor boy, he must be soaking wet!'

Now Rajoo had to fold his umbrella and go into the room with his wet and muddy boots. 'Good evening, Madam. Good evening, Sir!'

'Well, Rajoo,' Mary asked, 'why did you take the trouble to come in this downpour?'

Rajoo could have replied, 'Madam, these are ordinary showers. But even if there was a deluge, as the Bible says there was in the time of Noah and his Ark, it wouldn't be able to stop me from coming to you.'

But, aloud, he only took out the two books and handed them over to Mary. 'I came to deliver these two books. The librarian sent them for you.'

Mary was thanking Rajoo, and David was casting sidelong glances at the amazing boy who had braved this torrential rain to deliver two books to his Madam.

'I'll take your leave, Madam.'

'Why, Rajoo, what's the hurry?' asked Mary, and suggested, 'You're soaking wet. I'll make you a cup of tea. You'll feel better.'

'No, thank you, Madam,' said Rajoo, getting hot under the collar. Since his eyes had glimpsed the plunging neckline of Mary's rather daring dress, and the upper slopes of the breasts that were visible, he was confused and flustered. 'I have to get home, Madam. It's getting late, Madam. My mother must be waiting for me, Madam!' And, walking backwards, he ran from there. This time he did not even pause to open the umbrella which remained closed, under his arm.

Watching him go, David was thoughtful and silent.

'Very sweet child,' said Mary and did not notice David's raised eyebrows at the mention of the word 'child'.

'Yes,' he agreed vaguely and then was lost in thought.

Mary continued, 'David, in every school, there are many teachers and many students. But, sometimes, it seems that there is only one teacher and only one student.'

But David was not listening to her. He was looking out, where Rajoo, with the closed umbrella under his arm, could be seen slowly walking into the distance, till his lonely figure dissolved in the mist and the rain.

11

The classes were over for the day. The boys had drifted to their homes or were back in their hostel, preparing to go for games. Only Rajoo stood, waiting outside the school gate. Waiting for what? Or for whom? He was not sure himself. Maybe it was because Madam was still inside talking to the principal and had not gone home. Every day, David came to escort her. But today he had not come so far, perhaps he was busy elsewhere. Or, Rajoo conjectured hopefully, he has gone away. In any case, he hoped to get a chance to walk along with Madam. He had even thought of some questions which he would ask her on the way—something about Wordsworth's attitude to nature as revealed in his poetry.

He was startled out of his reverie as a voice greeted him from behind. 'Hello, Rajoo!' The bundle of books and notebooks fell from his hands.

David! How tall he was, how well-built, he looked very smart in a blue pullover. In his imagination, Rajoo compared David to himself—the shortish, plumpish, uncouth boy.

'Hello, Sir.' Rajoo was confused and flustered as he bent down to pick up his books. David helped him with the scattered books and, as he picked up a notebook, out came an amateurishly drawn portrait of Mary, one with red and blue pencils, enclosed with a valentine heart with the pencilled inscription in ornamental lettering, 'TO MADAM WITH LOVE!' Even before Rajoo snatched it away from him, David had seen what it was—a gift which was being prepared for the approaching St. Valentine's Day.

'Is the school over?' David asked to keep the conversation going.

'Yes, Sir, it's all over.' Having collected his books, Rajoo wanted to go away, but somehow be couldn't.

David noted the boy's predicament, and asked with an understanding smile, 'Are you waiting for someone?'

'Yes, Sir—No, Sir—I will be getting along, Sir—goodbye, Sir, goodbye!'

Just then Mary came out and (Rajoo noted with dismay) visibly brightened at the sight of David.

'Sorry, David, you had to wait so long, dar ...' She did not complete the word 'darling' as she saw Rajoo who seemed to be walking backwards.

'Hello, Rajoo,' she called out, 'you haven't gone home yet?'

'I am going, right now ...' He spoke in utter confusion. 'Goodbye, Madam, goodbye, Sir.' And then he ran from there and dared not look back, for he knew he would be watched.

David and Mary walked through a shady avenue, their arms encircling each other's waists.

'Poor Rajoo!' David said sympathetically.

'Don't you pity him!' Mary quickly said. 'He is a most mischievous fellow. Always up to some trick. But he is a darling.'

'Darling?' David repeated.

'Yes, darling—not only of his class but of the whole school, the students as well as the staff.'

'He may be the darling of the whole school,' said David, slowly, thoughtfully, 'but he wants to be the darling of his Madam only.'

'David, what are you saying?'

'I am talking sense, Mary. I think that your Joker has hopelessly fallen in love.'

'Fallen in love!' Mary innocently asked though she knew what the answer would be. 'But with whom?'

'With his teacher, with his Madam!'

'You mean me! Don't be silly, David.' Mary was vexed with the suggestion, which sounded ugly to her. 'A boy of hardly fourteen or fifteen—what does he know of love? Are you joking or irrationally jealous of a mere child?'

'No, Mary, I am not joking, I am serious. This is a dangerous age. Boys of fifteen or sixteen are hungry for love—wherever they find some understanding, some sympathy, they are liable to fall in love.'

Mary stopped. Now she was really worried. 'Could it be true,' she thought, as she leaned against a tree.

'But, David, how do you know what is in the heart of that poor boy?'

David looked into the depths of her brown eyes and his voice seemed to come from deep down in his heart. 'Because once upon a time I, too, was fifteen years old!'

'And now?' Mary teased him with mischief in her eyes.

'Now, again I am fifteen years old,' David replied and took a step towards her. Now she could feel his hot breath on her cheeks. '… And have fallen in love with a twenty-one-year-old teacher!'

'Liar!' said Mary, and her lips remained invitingly half-open.

'It's the truth,' he said and came still nearer. Now they were separated just by a breath.

'Can you give some proof?' she asked, her eyes closed but a tantalizing smile on her lips.

'Yes,' said David, and closed her mouth with his lips. Now it was no longer possible for her to say anything. Then they kissed each other, and seemed to relish the taste, and kissed each other again. Rajoo and his fifteen-year-old love were forgotten!

Rajoo, who was watching from behind a tree, could not endure it any longer. Mortified and tormented, he ran from there as if those demons were still pursuing him, as indeed they were!

12

It was the students versus staff hockey match, watched with great excitement by all the boys and teachers of the school. Mary was playing centre forward in the staff team, and she was playing very well. At least Rajoo thought so, as he watched and followed with his eyes her every movement. It seemed that he had telescopic lenses fitted to his eyes which were constantly focused on Mary, as she ran with the ball from one end of the field to the other. He was so engrossed in watching Mary that he did not notice that someone had come and sat down by his side. But when an ice cream choc-o-bar suddenly appeared before his eyes, he had to look around.

'Hello, Rajoo!' David again!

'Hello, Sir!' he greeted him without enthusiasm.

'Ice cream?' David again offered the choc-o-bar which Rajoo accepted with some reluctance. He thanked David and went on watching the game which was in an exciting phase, Mary charging across the field, dribbling the ball with her hockey stick.

'Good, isn't it?' David asked.

'Yes, she's very good, Sir,' replied Rajoo, without taking his eyes off Mary who was now nearing the goal.

'I am talking about the ice cream.'

'And I thought you were talking about—' Rajoo just checked himself blurting out the name, as he looked back at David.

'Did you think I was talking about Mary?' And then, without waiting for a confirmation, he added, 'Better eat your choc-o-bar, or it will melt.'

'It is very good. I like all kinds of ice cream.'

'I know.'

'Who told you?'

'Mary.'

'Oh! Madam!'

'She also told me that when you grow up, you don't want to be a doctor, engineer or barrister, but that you want to be a joker, to make people laugh.'

Suddenly, Rajoo got up. He suspected David was making fun of him, trying to humiliate him. 'Then you, too, make fun of me, as all the others do, calling me Joker! Joker! Joker!'

Rajoo was now shouting, and the disturbed spectators were looking at him angrily, hissing 'Shshsh!' David caught him by the arm, and gently led him away. 'Come with me. We'll go out in the garden and have a man-to-man talk.'

Rajoo looked up gratefully. He was tired of being

treated as a child, and approved of anyone who referred to him as a man!

Now they were sitting on a park bench and talking like two friends, man to man.

David said, 'Rajoo, do you know how many great men in the world have been laughed at and ridiculed as jokers?'

Rajoo shook his head. 'No, I don't know. Who were they?'

'To begin with, there was Jesus Christ. The Romans called Him a charlatan and a magician—till they nailed him on the cross. And yet he only blessed his tormentors and his murderers. Wasn't that a joke, the gesture of a divinely inspired joker?'

'Who else?' Now Rajoo was getting interested in these divinely inspired jokers.

'Then there was Mahatma Gandhi whom the Englishmen called a half-naked fakir. The cartoonists depicted him as Mickey Mouse. He was shot four times through his heart, yet, as he breathed his last, there was no anger or hatred in his heart. He just took the name of God, said, "Hey Ram!" and died. Wasn't that the gesture of a joker who was divinely inspired?'

Rajoo had seen the picture of Mahatma Gandhi on a calendar. A small, thin, darkish man. Very big ears. Small eyes peering through the round glasses of steel-rimmed spectacles. A loincloth, and bare above the waist. On his head he had a funny-looking bamboo hat, like the ones Bengali peasants wear during the monsoon. Looked like a joker. In the picture there was a child, too, who was dragging the Mahatma by catching hold of his bamboo staff. The child and the Mahatma were both laughing, making each other laugh.

'So Gandhiji, too, was a joker! Who else?'

'Then there was Chacha Nehru, who stood on his head every day, so that he could view the topsy-turvy world correctly. Wasn't that the gesture of a great joker who, too, makes himself ridiculous to appreciate the ridiculousness of life?'

'But what have these great ones of the world got to do with insignificant me,' thought Rajoo. Aloud he said, 'I am sorry, I have not understood you; what exactly do you want to say?'

David gave him a friendly pat on the back before answering. 'Only this—that the clown, or the joker, is not an ordinary man. He looks foolish, but that is only the mask of a clown. He is sensitive to both pain and pleasure. He is the one who pours every joy and sorrow of life into his laughter. At heart he is a child—whether he is fifteen years old or fifty.'

Rajoo did not understand all the philosophical subtleties, but he thought he had an inkling of what David was trying to say.

'Rajoo,' David was now summing up, 'in this world, there are too many purveyors of pain and anguish and sorrow, let there be at least one man who distributes the gift of laughter. I think you can be that man.'

'I?' Rajoo asked, surprised.

'Yes, you,' David said, looking straight into his eyes. 'But for that you'll have to suffer much. You will be heartbroken, and yet you'll smile, you'll laugh, and make others laugh. You will be heartbroken, and yet you will love, for you are in love with love; for you the act of loving, like laughing, like making others laugh, is an end in itself.'

Rajoo was silent, trying to understand, and assimilate, what David had said.

Then David asked him, 'So now that you know your destiny, you won't resent being called a joker?'

Rajoo wanted to say a lot, but he couldn't find words to express what he was feeling, what he was thinking. So he said nothing, only raised his right hand and said aloud, '*Mera naam* Joker!'

When the match ended, their team having won, Mary looked all round for David. Someone told her he was sitting on a park bench, talking to Rajoo.

'Hello, David,' she said as she saw him. He was alone.

'Hello, Mary. Congratulations.'

'Thanks,' she said, looking around. 'Where's Rajoo? Someone told me he was sitting here, talking to you.'

David looked up at the sky. 'He was sitting here by my side. But now he's gone, far beyond me.'

13

He was getting ready to go to school when Rajoo heard his mother's rasping cough.

'Ma, how are you feeling?' he asked, putting the books in his satchel.

'I am all right, Son,' she said, and had another asthmatic fit.

Rajoo went up to her and touched her forehead. He cried out in alarm, 'Ma, you are burning with fever; I won't let you go to work.'

Using all her willpower to suppress her coughing,

she tried to get up. 'If I don't go to work, from where will the ration come? How shall we pay your next term's fees?'

'Ma, you have worked enough. Now your son is grown up. Let him work. You must rest.' He forced her to lie down.

'Have you gone mad?' she protested. 'If you start working, how will you go to school? And if you won't study, how will you become a man of consequence? How will my dreams come true?'

'Don't worry, Ma. I will work as well as study.'

'You're still a child. What kind of work can you do?'

'Ma, I will take up any job that I can get.'

Rajoo did get a job after his own heart. It required him to dress up as a joker—a clown's tall cap, clown's loose dress, painted face—and collect a crowd by ringing a bell, and then sell powdered antimony for the eyes. Rajoo had observed the way street magicians, snake charmers and the bunder-walas spoke in rapidfire bursts, and he adapted the same technique to collect and hold crowds of would-be buyers of his Naintara soorma.

'*Hindu ko Ram Ram, Musalman ko salaam,*

Christaan ko good morning aur Sardarji ko sat sri akal. Friends, comrades and Indians. Can you guess what is that thing that reads the Vedas, and also the Quran Shareef, the Holy Bible and the Granth Saheb, which sees the Taj Mahal of Agra and also the Birla Mandir of Delhi, which sees the holy sangam of Ganga, Jamna and the mythical Saraswati at Allahabad, and also sees the *Sangam* of Raj Kapoor, Rajendra Kumar and Vyjayantimala? Speak up, speak up, what is that wondrous, fabulous, priceless object?'

Everyone was puzzled, silent. How could there be such a thing?

A Sardarji spoke up in Punjabi, '*Ohe, tu hi das na.*' You tell us!

'So you admit defeat, you wise ones?'

'Yes, yes,' a bald man replied, scratching his head.

'That thing is not one but two—our eyes! Don't they read the Vedas, as well as all the other holy books?'

People laughed and shook their heads. They listened attentively to whatever he was going to say.

Now he began some real, glib sales talk (mimicking a medicine-seller whom he had heard and watched).

'Gentle folk, kind folk, wise folk, foolish folk, this folk, that folk, remember: your eyes are God's greatest gift to you. Preserve them, protect them, safeguard them against the glare of the sun, against the dust and dirt and smoke that fills the air of our cities. If your eyes are watering, if they are red, if they are sore, if they are strained, or if you are squint-eyed so that you seem to be winking at pretty girls and their brothers and fiancés threaten to beat you up …'

And he mimed a squint-eyed man and then winked so outrageously that the spectators burst out laughing—he knew now that he could be a professional joker, he knew how to make people laugh!

'In short, if you have any ocular, visual, optic, opthalmic trouble; if you want to be clear-eyed, clear-sighted, far-sighted, keen-eyed, eagle-eyed, hawk-eyed; to be able to stare, gaze, leer, ogle and glare at your beloved, the apple of your eyes, sometimes it also becomes the apple of discord—then use only Naintara toothpowder …'

The deliberate mistake again sent the crowd into peals of laughter—he *could* make people laugh!

'… No, no, sorry, not Naintara toothpowder but Naintara eye-powder. One rupee for a small bottle. Two rupees for a big bottle. Take your choice, friends, we have very limited stocks. First come first served … Here you are, here you are …'

Now he knew the secret of a joker's success. He

must continue to wear the mask of a fool, to talk like a fool, to seem to make mistakes like a fool, and to have the clumsy mannerisms of a fool!

The eye-powder was selling like hot cakes. People crowded round Rajoo, blocking the road for a big black car that had to be braked to a stop.

In the car was seated a fat, rich woman and her son, a boy in school uniform.

'What's all this? A riot or something?' The fat woman commanded the chauffeur to find out.

The driver looked out of the window and reported, 'It is a street hawker selling medicines.'

'Mummy, this is a boy from our school,' said the boy by her side, and then started shouting, 'Rajoo! Eh, Rajoo!'

Rajoo turned around and saw his class fellow, Govind, sitting in the car. 'Hello, Govind,' he said, going up to the car. 'Call out my proxy in class. I may be a little late.'

'Driver!' the woman ordered, reacting to Rajoo's clownish attire, with evident distaste, 'drive on. Never mind the crowd.'

The car leapt forward, missing a couple of pedestrians who shouted a few curses and obscenities. Then she turned to her son, 'Is it true that this—this street joker—is your classmate?'

'Yes, Mummy,' Govind replied with enthusiasm, 'very interesting fellow. Full of amusing tricks. We all call him Joker. He is a poor boy, so he has to do some work to earn while he learns. Isn't he wonderful, Mummy?'

'Yes,' hissed the woman, 'it is, indeed, wonderful that such a boy should be in the same school as you are.'

14

When he joined the class, the boys informed Rajoo that he had been summoned by the principal.

Rajoo felt nervous as perhaps his habitual late-coming had been discovered and reported to the principal. On the way, he kept thinking of an effective excuse or alibi when he saw Govind's mother emerging from the office. Rajoo greeted her by joining his hands in a respectful namaskar. The rich, fat woman snubbed him with a disdainful look. But even then Rajoo never imagined that there was any connection between her visit to the principal's office and his being summoned there.

Inside, under a portrait of Christ sat the bearded padre who acted as the principal of the Convent of Jesus School. But much of Rajoo's nervousness was dispelled when he saw the reassuring presence of Mary. 'Not much harm can come to me,' he thought, 'so long as Madam is here.' She gave him a comforting smile, and he felt greatly encouraged.

The principal looked up from some papers and said, 'Raj Ranbir?'

'Yes, Sir.'

Again he consulted the papers. 'You have not paid your fees for the last three months?'

Before he could reply, Mary interjected, 'Sir, haven't I told you I will be responsible for his arrears?'

Rajoo looked at her with gratitude, but he had no intention of being obliged to anyone, not even Madam. But the principal silenced Mary's interruption with a curt 'Miss Mary, I am talking to Rajoo'.

Now Rajoo had to explain. 'Sir—the fact is—Sir, my mother is very ill—that's why we have not seen able to pay off the arrears ...'

The principal banged the table and raised his voice to an angry pitch. 'And that is why you put on a joker's dress and go about distributing advertisement handbills and selling medicines on the streets?'

Rajoo not only admitted to his 'crime' but did so enthusiastically. 'Yes, Sir, I like to become a joker, to make people laugh. My father was also a joker!' He smiled at the vision of his father.

But the smile disappeared from his face when he heard the principal say, 'Raj, I am sorry, you will have to leave the school.'

Rajoo could only mutter, 'Yes, Sir?' Two words, but there was so much in them—surprise, regret, pain and sorrow, a question and an indictment.

Mary pleaded on behalf of Rajoo. 'Sir, Raj Ranbir is an intelligent and bright boy. To dress up like a joker and to distribute handbills is no crime. In America, thousands of students earn while they learn.'

'But this is not America, Miss Mary. This is India,' said the principal, defending his decision. 'I have to consider the opinions of other parents. Some of them don't want their sons to sit in the same classroom as a street hawker or joker. Mrs Verma has just been here. You know how angry and upset she was?'

'Mrs Verma?' Rajoo thought. Govind's mummy. That fat, rich woman, in a Benarasi brocade-border sari, who had snubbed him as she went out. So that's the reason why she had come here. That's the reason why he was being turned out of school. The non-payment of fees was only an excuse! He was so full of resentment and anger that he didn't pay attention to what was being said—till the principal said to Mary: 'Don't you worry. I will get Raj admitted to a charity school. Remind me to speak to Father Lobo.'

'Thank you, Sir,' Raj said slowly but decisively, his voice tinged with bitterness. 'But I am not going to study in a charity school. Don't take the trouble of talking to Father Lobo. Thank you, Sir.' He left the room, his head held high.

The principal and Mary watched Rajoo as he walked out. The room suddenly seemed empty and desolate and dark. It seemed as if, with Rajoo, the light had gone out of that room for ever.

Mary, too, now got up. 'I am sorry, Sir. Rajoo being turned out like this will not please Him.'

'Him? Whom?' The principal was puzzled.

Mary silently pointed to the portrait of Christ and said, 'Him!' Then she walked out of the room.

Outside, in an alcove in the corridor, against the background of stained-glass windows, stood a marble statue of Christ. At that moment, it appeared to have an expression of compassion for the boy who was now bidding farewell to Him.

'Goodbye, Sir,' Rajoo was saying. 'They have turned out your joker from the school. Is it because *he* wanted to make you laugh, and *they* want to keep you sad, always?'

Rajoo thought, 'Am I imagining it? Is it a trick of the light? Or do I see a faint, sad little smile on the stone lips of Christ?'

He heard Mary's voice. 'Rajoo!'

'Yes, Madam!' he replied without turning to look at her. He did not want her to see the tears in his eyes. 'I am going away, Madam.'

'Rajoo, I am going away, too.'

'You, too? Why? Because of me?'

'No, Rajoo.' And now Mary was diffident about saying what she had to. 'In a few days I'm getting married.'

Marriage! The word had the impact of a flash of lightning. Rajoo felt his heartbeat stop—but this must be only his imagination. If his heart had really stopped beating, he would have instantly fallen dead. But at that moment he knew that there is another kind of death, too. It occurs when a fifteen-year-old boy finds that his dreams, his hopes, his happiness have all died suddenly. Still he was alive, standing there, hearing, feeling. Why am I alive? Why am I forced to live? Why? What for? For what purpose? He had no answer to these questions—yet!

Within a second he felt all this, he thought all this, and then the confusion of his thoughts crystallized into a question mark. He asked, 'With David?' though he need not have asked.

'Yes,' answered Mary. 'The wedding will take place in the local cathedral. David wants you to be best man.'

'Best man?' He hadn't heard the expression before. 'What's that, Madam?'

'The dearest and the best friend is called best man. You will come, won't you?'

And now Rajoo gulped down his tears and brought a smile to his face. 'Yes, Madam, I will be there.'

Then, reluctant to turn his eyes away, he started walking backwards—he was moving away from Mary, or Mary was going away from him!—till he stumbled against a stand with a flower vase, recovered in time, steadied the vase and the stand and saved them from falling. His gestures, his movements, even in the moment of doom, were clumsy and comical, and brought an involuntary smile to the face of Mary. Looking at her, he realized that he was a joker after all; he was a joker above all! Then he, too, smiled embarrassedly and said, 'Goodbye, Madam.'

When he was gone, Mary breathed out a long-drawn-out sigh from the depths of her heart. 'Oh, Rajoo, my dear, why could you not be five years older?'

15

Mary and David were married in the cathedral with all the colourful ceremonial of the Catholic Church. The bride and bridegroom exchanged rings and the officiating priest blessed the couple. In the presence of all the boys and teachers of the school—in the presence of Rajoo—David and Mary were pronounced man and wife.

The big church bell in the belfry began to toll, chiming the happy tidings.

And, like the Hunchback of Notre-Dame (whose story he had read and whose role he had played in the school play), it was Rajoo who was pulling the rope that rang the happy bell, while his own heart was breaking. But he knew that the same church bell also tolls for the death of a parishioner. Today, a part of him had died. Was the church bell proclaiming the death of his childhood?

When David and Mary came out of the church, they were showered with rose petals and confetti. Two rows of their friends and colleagues stood by to offer them congratulations.

They were coming down the steps, bowing, shaking hands, receiving congratulations, offering thanks, but their eyes were searching for Rajoo who had silently come and joined the group of schoolboys.

He saw the bridal couple coming towards him. How tall, dark and handsome David was in his black suit with a white carnation in his buttonhole. Mary, in her white wedding gown, looked like a veritable fairy who would soon fly away with her handsome bridegroom. Rajoo swallowed the lump in his throat to utter the formalities.

'Congratulations, Mr David; congratulations, Madam.'

After formal thanks, David asked Rajoo, 'Aren't you going to kiss the bride?'

Rajoo flushed scarlet as the blood rushed to his cheeks; he felt giddy and feverish. He could not speak.

Mary, coming forward, smilingly offered her cheek, and David encouraged Rajoo. 'As the best man, it is your right—and your duty!'

Feeling awkward and embarrassed, Rajoo pecked at the cheek with his burning lips and then stood away, looking down. It was the briefest contact, but from that moment his consciousness was filled with the fragrance of Mary—the sweet smell of a ripe, young, healthy body—for years to come.

Mary signalled to a bridesmaid and she brought

forward a box gift-wrapped in colourful paper. She gave it to David, and David gave it to Rajoo.

Rajoo, surprised, said, 'But I should have given you a present.'

'Young man, you've given me the best present of all—' said David, and smilingly pointed to Mary, '—your teacher!'

Unwrapping the parcel, Rajoo asked, 'But what is this?'

'This is you,' said Mary as the little joker came out of the wrapping.

Rajoo sadly looked at the doll and asked, 'What shall I do with it?'

David placed a friendly hand on the boy's shoulder. 'Keep it with you. It will remind you of the destiny of a clown.'

In that moment, Rajoo remembered all that David had told him about the divinely ordained jokers.

Now Mary was telling him, pointing to the doll, 'Keep it with you. Give it to the one who deserves it. Goodbye, Rajoo. God bless you.'

'Goodbye, Madam.'

'Goodbye, Rajoo.'

'Goodbye, David.'

Smiling, radiant, and yet a little sad at the moment of parting, David and Mary got into the decorated car. There was a shower of confetti, and the school band struck the wedding march.

And so, Mary went out of Rajoo's life.

Did she go away for good, forever?

No. In his heart of hearts, Rajoo knew it was not forever, that she would come back to him at least one more time. When? Where? How?

She had gone, but she had given him back the little joker, who was his faith, and the memory of his father.

Rajoo now walked alone on the road of life. His feet were on the ground, but his head was in the clouds. In his eyes were the tears that he would have to learn to hide. In his heart was the promise of a joker's life. And in his hand dangled the little joker, an amused look in his eyes, a wistful smile on his lips, as he looked ahead to the days that were not yet born.

Part Two

THE FAIRY AND THE FOOL ON A FLYING TRAPEZE

1

Rajoo drifted from place to place, along with his mother, two gypsies ever on the move. The boy grew into a young man, the young man into a man. The struggle for life, the privations and the deprivations that he endured had lined his face with deeply etched creases. But that little joker remained the same as he was—ageless, indestructible. 'I should try to be the same,' Rajoo often thought. 'Whatever my age, whatever my pain and my suffering, I should always be laughing, and making others laugh.'

He laughed and made others laugh, occasionally getting temporary odd jobs, distributing leaflets, or dressed as a joker, entertaining children with peep shows in carnivals. Wherever he went, the little ones would recognize him and cry out with delight, 'Joker! Joker!'

And Rajoo would acknowledge the greeting with joy and with pride. He would laugh to make them laugh by tripping himself and falling. The children would clap their hands and shout, 'Joker! Joker!'

2

When he arrived in Bombay, Rajoo asked where he could get a job. Someone pointed to the Employment Exchange. 'That is where you will find a job.'

After waiting in the queue, Rajoo at last managed to get inside and reach the counter.

'Name?' the clerk filling a form asked.

'*Mera naam* Joker. They call me a clown—but you can call me Rajoo!'

'Age?'

'The yogi and the joker don't have any particular age!'

'Education?'

'I have been turned out of several schools.'

The clerk did not appreciate the philosophy—or the humour—of these answers. He bluntly asked, 'What kind of work can you do?'

'I can sing, I can cry, I can laugh, I can make others laugh, I can make *you* laugh.'

But the serious-faced clerk did not smile as he asked, 'To make people laugh—what kind of work is it?'

'This is the only worthwhile occupation, mister; the rest is all money making drudgery!'

'You talk like a clown—then go to some circus.

There is no job for you here.' The clerk dismissed him, and asked the next man in the queue to come forward.

That evening when Rajoo reached the chawl where, in one room, he lived with his mother, he found her lying on a cot, too ill and weak to get up.

She recognized the footsteps of her son and opened her eyes. 'Did you get a job?'

'I found it but did not get it.' He tried to avoid a direct answer which might add to her disappointment. Then he casually said, treating it as a joke: 'Who would give a real job to your worthless, uneducated son? Everyone says, "The circus is the place for folks like you."'

'Circus?' The sick old woman reacted with a look of alarm and sat up with some difficulty. There was anger and bitterness in her voice. 'Again you're thinking of joining the circus?' Then she melted into tears. 'Promise me, my son. Do anything—sweep the streets or carry loads like a coolie, but never think of becoming a clown in a circus.' After so many years, she was as adamant as ever on this issue.

But Rajoo had got tired of his life of casual employment—two days of work, five days of idleness. He thought his mother, realizing his difficulties, would relent. 'If I don't work in the circus,' he now said with some impatience, 'where shall we find money to eat, to buy medicines for you?'

The old woman got up on her wobbly legs, slowly came to her son and, clasping him to her bosom, said, 'I don't want medicines to save my life. I want a long life for my son. I don't want him, like his father, to leave me to suffer alone in this world.'

Rajoo felt moved by his mother's tearful pleading. He reassured her, 'Don't worry, Ma. I won't join the circus, I won't join any circus!'

But all the time, behind the mother's back, his eyes were focused on the cupboard where the little joker, the symbol of his father, was seated in a corner, biding his time, and beckoning Rajoo with his lifeless glass eyes.

It was a chance or his own destiny, or the memory of his father, that directed Rajoo's footsteps towards the Big Top of a circus on Bombay's Azad Maidan. But one morning he found himself jostling in a crowd of the idle and the curious that stood in front of the entrance.

'There are many hours still, even for the matinee show,' wondered Rajoo. 'Then why this big crowd? What are they waiting for?' When he asked a man in the crowd, he was informed that a party of foreign circus artistes was expected, and the Indian circus people were going to give them a reception.

Only then did Rajoo notice the legend inscribed in big, bold letters on a streamer strung above the main gate: 'WELCOME SOVIET ARTISTES'.

Rajoo had heard of the Soviet Union, though most people called it by its old name—Russia. He had heard that it was a big country, a great country, and that they had a government of peasants and workers. But he had read somewhere that in Russia, people neither laughed nor smiled, that they had no entertainment, but only talked of the Revolution and Communism. He did not know if they had even one circus in the Soviet Union. And now here were Soviet artistes arriving to perform in an Indian circus! Among them must be a Russian clown, too. Does he make the Russian people laugh in the same way that Indian jokers make Indian spectators laugh—as he, Rajoo, would make them laugh if he got a chance? And, in that crowd waiting in the morning sun, Rajoo had a comforting vision of Indian clowns and Russian clowns, American clowns and Chinese clowns, German clowns and French clowns, and clowns of all the other countries, making their respective people laugh, and combining to make the people of the entire world laugh. Could the laughing people hate each other and wage wars and drop atom bombs on each other? No, they couldn't. Rajoo was quite sure of it.

They would have no time to do so. They would be too busy laughing to think of killing each other.

Rajoo was jerked out of this noonday reverie by the arrival of the Air India bus. One by one, the Russians came out. They were all fair-complexioned, athletic young men and pretty young women; some were blonde and some were black-haired. Many blonde ones had blue eyes—but then, Rajoo reminded himself, he had blue eyes, too. Now came out a Russian artiste, of about the same height as Rajoo, and the way he took off his hat and bowed to the bystanders, with extravagant and comical courtesy, it was apparent that he was the clown. So the Russians, too, had clowns and jokers who laughed and made others laugh! Just like the Indians? Just like any other human being?

The last to come out of the bus was a delicate blond Russian beauty. She was wearing a short skirt, and hesitated to jump down from the bus. A hefty man detached himself from the welcoming group of Indians ('That's Sher Singh, the famous ringmaster,' Rajoo's neighbour in the crowd whispered to him!) and rushed to her rescue. He lifted her in his arms as if she were a weightless doll, put her down, and received the reward of a grateful smile and a few words of thanks in incomprehensible Russian. When the girl in the short skirt passed near Rajoo, he gaped at her, spellbound by her beauty. Rajoo heard the old melody rising within him. It was the same music that he had heard when, years ago as a boy, he had first seen Mary. Will this one create the same disturbance in his life? No, no. How could that be? She was a foreigner, a Russian, while Rajoo was an Indian. She was obviously a celebrated artiste, while he was just a nameless man in the crowd. Even if he met her, he wouldn't know in what language to talk to her.

The tall, dark and handsome Mahender, the proprietor of the circus, who was also a renowned trapeze artiste, now signalled to his bevy of girls, in glittering Indian costumes, who were waiting with garlands in their hands. They proceeded to offer a typical Indian welcome to each of the arriving guests, garlanding him or her, and placing the auspicious red kumkum dot on the forehead. When that Russian fairy, too, was garlanded and a red bindi applied to her forehead, Rajoo felt her transformed into an Indian beauty. To have a closer and better look at her, he elbowed his way through the crowd and emerged in front, where the welcome ceremony was being performed.

When all the Russian artistes had been garlanded, one of the Indian girls noticed that they had forgotten to welcome one Russian who was still without a garland. Fair, blue-eyed, wearing loose-fitting pants and jacket, with an old hat on his head, the poor man seemed to be waiting for his turn. So the girl placed the remaining garland round his neck, applied the kumkum to his forehead, and went ahead. She did not notice the bewildered look on Rajoo's face. The rest of the Russian group had gone into the circus tent, and now this 'Russian', too, stepped in that direction. Almost immediately he stumbled and fell. The Pathan watchman who had been keeping back the surging crowd, rushed to the discomfited foreigner. Helping him to his feet, dusting his clothes, the Pathan solicitously asked in his mixed Punjabi-Hindi, 'Saheb, I hope you are not hurt.'

The watchman was surprised to hear the 'foreigner' answer him in Hindi, '*Koi baat naheen, Khan Saheb.*' It does not matter, Khan Saheb! Saying this, he was gone, leaving the watchman wondering how this, Russian spoke Hindi just like Indians. By the time it dawned on the simple-minded Pathan that someone had made a fool of him, the charlatan had already disappeared behind the flap of the tent. 'By God,' thought the watchman, 'I will teach him a lesson!' And he ran in to catch the culprit.

3

In the ring-shaped arena of the now empty circus, Mahender was talking to that Russian fairy through an interpreter, a Hindi-speaking Russian who had come with the group from Moscow.

Pointing to the garland and the red mark on her forehead, Mahender said, 'This is our Indian way for welcoming our foreign friends.'

When it was translated for her, she smiled. '*Kraseeva. Ochin Kraseeva.*'

'What did she say?' Mahender asked the interpreter.

'Beautiful. Very beautiful,' he interpreted for him.

'You, too, are very beautiful,' said the gallant Mahender to the girl.

When this was translated, she smiled again. '*Passiba.*'

'Thank you,' the interpreter translated.

'Tell Miss Marina,' said Mahender, 'that I have heard a lot about her. It will be an honour and a pleasure to do a trapeze act with her!'

In the adjacent large tent which was used for rehearsals, the Russian artistes were busy supervising the placing of their equipment, and among them the

Pathan watchman was searching for the gatecrasher who had pretended to be a Russian.

From a distance, he saw a man of the same medium height, wearing the same kind of clothes and hat, standing in a corner. Even though he could see only the back, the watchman was certain that it was the villain. Walking fast through the clusters of the Russian artistes, the Pathan reached the culprit and placed a heavy hand on his guilty shoulders.

'Eh, you fooled me to come inside under false pretences. Get out!'

The man resented the watchman's rude gesture, and loudly protested in some language incomprehensible to the Pathan. This brought other Russian artistes who all began to speak together. Now the poor watchman was nonplussed. Had he made another mistake, threatened to oust a genuine Russian? But he looked the same—the same clothes, the same hat, the same blue eyes. Then why was everyone so excited?

The noisy hubbub brought Mahender, the proprietor, to the scene. 'What's it? What has happened?' he asked the interpreter.

The interpreter, speaking his bookish Hindi, tried to reassure him. 'It is nothing, really.' Pointing to the watchman, he added, 'This comrade is labouring under some misapprehension.'

Mahender shouted at his watchman. 'What kind of misbehaviour is this? How dare you insult our guests?'

The Pathan had realized his mistake. 'I'm sorry, Sir. I was looking for an intruder who had fooled me by looking like a Russian!'

Mahender severely reprimanded him, 'You fool. Can't you see the big difference between a Russian and an Indian?'

The Pathan who had been fooled by the fair complexion, the blue eyes and the clothes worn by the intruder now said, not to contradict his boss, but to explain his mistake, 'It's not a very big difference, Sir.' The simple fellow did not know that he had uttered a profound statement. There was no difference between a Russian and an Indian, between man and man!

Mahender was feeling embarrassed that one of the servants had unwittingly insulted the guests within minutes of their arrival. He warned the Pathan, 'Remember now, these are our very special guests. They should not have any cause to complain. Now, I want you to go to each of them and beg their forgiveness.'

The watchman joined his hands and, first of all, addressed the shortish man in the old hat. 'Saheb, please forgive me. I will never make such a mistake again.'

This was translated by the interpreter to the Russian who was, obviously, a clown, the way he doffed his hat and bowed to the watchman, and even embraced him, to proclaim that all was forgiven and forgotten.

While the watchman was going from one Russian to another, and asking for their forgiveness, each one smilingly shaking hands with him, Mahender was walking away with the interpreter. 'Look here, Brother Rybakov. Tell your comrades not to mind it if there is some misunderstanding. But, otherwise, if they have any difficulty or problem, they should immediately get in touch with me—through you, of course.'

They were now passing near a number of circus props—and, among them, a big inverted basket. When they passed by, the basket slowly lifted itself and Rajoo emerged from under it. He still had the garland round his neck and the red mark on his forehead. After shaking hands with the other Russians, the watchman came to him. When he had been ordered to apologize to every single Russian, why should he leave out even one?

Automatically shaking hands with Rajoo, the Pathan said, 'Excuse me, Saheb, such a mistake will never be repeated.'

This time Rajoo did not repeat his earlier mistake of speaking in Hindi, and spoke in Russian-sounding gibberish but made clear by his pantomime gestures that he, too, believed in forgiving and forgetting.

4

The circus auditorium was still lying deserted, but there was much activity in the arena, where Indian and Soviet artistes were going to rehearse together for the first time.

Mahender had changed to trapeze tights over which he was wearing a dressing gown. He had just come out of his tent when he was accosted by Sher Singh, the ringmaster.

'Mahender Saheb!'

'Yes, Sher Singh. Won't it be exciting to rehearse with the Soviet artistes? Marina, I am told, is great on the trapeze.'

'Mahender Saheb,' Sher Singh said in a sulky tone, 'your Sher Singh, too, is not an ordinary ringmaster.'

'There is no doubt about it,' agreed Mahender and wondered what was coming next.

'I hear some Russian ringmaster is going to perform tonight with my lions …'

'Yes, but ...'

'Now, look here, Mahender Saheb. I have been working with you for many years. I cannot tolerate any other ringmaster performing with my lions.'

'Sher Singh, the Russian ringmaster is our guest. We must give him a chance to perform with our animals, since he can't bring his own.'

'But where is he?' Sher Singh asked. 'I don't see any ringmaster among the Russian artistes.'

'He is coming by another plane along with his bears. Or, maybe he has come already.'

'Bears are altogether different,' Sher Singh bragged. 'There are many bears in their country. But this Russian can never face my lions. I tell you, he will be so frightened of them that he may never come!'

'Then you have nothing to worry about. If he doesn't come, naturally you will perform. Okay?' And then he walked away for the rehearsal with Marina.

But Sher Singh, left alone, was struck with a disturbing thought, 'And if he *does* come?'

Hidden behind the curtains, Rajoo was watching the combined rehearsal of the Indian and Soviet circus artistes. 'These Russian girls,' he thought, 'are real daredevils.' A red-headed beauty was swinging upside down from a trapeze bar, without any net or any other protection. A Central Asian brunette was walking—rather, dancing to the rhythm of the music—on a tight rope. Other girls were doing somersaults, or intricate acrobatics, as if they had rubber bones in their bodies. All around many different items were being rehearsed simultaneously, and it was difficult to say who was an Indian and who was a Russian.

Rajoo saw Mahender walk in and look around to see that the rehearsals were proceeding satisfactorily. Then he flung his dressing gown aside. From head to foot, his taut, athletic body was outlined by the trapeze costume. How broad his chest was, how muscular his biceps! Twice he raised his arms, bent and touched his toes, and there wasn't the slightest bend in his knee joints.

And Rajoo remembered an occasion, many years ago, when he was fifteen years old and studying in a convent school. In the drill period, he was trying to bend down just like that when his short pants had split at the stitches in the back, and he had to abandon the drill. How ashamed he had been to admit before the lady teacher that his pant was torn! At that time he did not even know her very well, still she had been very kind and considerate. How nice was his teacher, his 'Madam' as they all called her! How beautiful!

Always friendly, and gay, teaching them how to sing, taking them to picnics. It was on such a picnic—even after so many years, he blushed at the vision of her graceful body. Where was she now? How was she? Had she become old and aged? But in his imagination she was just as young and as beautiful and her face and her body were just as disturbingly beautiful …

He had thought of Mary, and here she was in that circus, coming towards him, in a blue dressing gown, carrying a little lap dog in her arms. How could it be Mary? Or was it his imagination playing tricks on him? When she came nearer, Rajoo saw that it was not Mary but that Russian fairy, whom he had seen before, and whom her colleagues called 'Marina'. She was not Mary. Mary had black hair, hers was golden brown. Mary had big black eyes, while she had light brown eyes. And yet both of them had something, some mysterious quality, some subtle shade of beauty that was common. Even the name 'Marina' was but a variation of Mary. Was it a mere coincidence? Or could there be some significance in this coincidence? Why did his heart beat faster at the sight of Marina as, once upon a time, it used to beat at the sight of Mary?

Why did his ears ring with the same old melody?

She came straight towards Rajoo. 'How does she know I'm standing here?' he thought. Rajoo greeted her by taking off his hat.

She said something in Russian (she evidently took him to be a member of the Russian group!) and then dumped the little dog in his arms, and walked off to the centre of the arena.

Rajoo saw her exchanging smiles with the rehearsing artistes before taking off her dressing gown. She wore a flaming red skintight trapeze costume. She didn't actually fly, but in a graceful and easy nonchalant way, she held a rope and allowed herself to be hauled up to the trapeze; it was, indeed, a fairy floating up in the air.

She stood with Mahender, high up on the trapeze platform. Every now and then, she would swing away, float over the arena, catch another dangling, swinging trapeze bar, and gracefully land on the opposite platform. Rajoo gaped in wonderment how one so delicate and fragile could be so recklessly daring!

While Rajoo was looking up, the little lap dog was getting restless. Once when Marina—or was it Mary?—swung and leaped through space to catch the other trapeze bar, Rajoo was so excited that he started to clap and cheer. As he opened his hands, the dog jumped down and ran away. Now Rajoo realized the significance of the proverb, 'If you love me, love my dog'. If he wanted to have another meeting with this Russian beauty, he would have to retrieve the dog. If the dog was lost, so were his chances of courting her.

Rajoo and the dog chased each other all over the backyard of the circus, but the dog was small and ran where Rajoo could not pursue him. The dog and Rajoo did a merry dance—through the elephants' stable, under the lions' cages, through the legs of the horses and the zebras, in and out of the tents of the circus personnel.

In one tent, while the dog sneaked under the flap and got out of the other side, Rajoo, too, followed him on all fours, and when he stood up he found himself surrounded by a bevy of Russian girl acrobats in various stages of dressing and undressing. He couldn't understand what they were screaming about, but he guessed they were making uncomplimentary remarks about the intruder. Miming his apologies, Rajoo made good his escape.

He was still running after the dog when he came across the Russian fairy who had, apparently, come down to earth to find her dog missing and, along with it, the man to whom she had entrusted it. As soon as she saw Rajoo, she began, fluently and rapidly, describing the dog with her hands, and uttering the word 'Sabaka! Sabaka!' over and over again.

'Sabaka,' Rajoo concluded, was Russian for dog. So he, too, said, 'Sabaka? You mean—' And he simulated the yelping sound of a little dog.

Marina said, 'Da—da' and at the same time nodded her head in the affirmative.

'Ah, your dog!' said Rajoo, pantomiming with his hands, pointing in opposite directions. 'It is a phantom. I tell you, a will o' the wisp. If I go here, he goes there, if I go there, he comes here. I am breathless with running, still I could not catch up with him.'

She said something in Russian and was going away, having decided perhaps to search for the dog on her own, when Rajoo called her.

'*Aji, suniye toh* ... Lady, please listen to me!' and when she stopped and turned round, he continued: 'May I tell you how wonderful you were on the trapeze! You fly in the air like a fairy.' Rajoo's hands fluttered like the wings of a bird—or a fairy!—and, unmindful of the fact that she was not understanding a word of what he was saying, he went on. 'Yes, just like a fairy—that's what you are! The fairy of my dreams and my mother's dreams.'

Marina shrugged her pretty shoulders to indicate that she had not understood what he was trying to say, but Rajoo was not one to be discouraged.

'Remember, milady, one day I, too, will work with you in the circus.' Pointing to the sky, and then to the earth, he said, 'If you will be high up there, I will be down below here. So, don't forget me. *Mera naam* Joker!'

'Joker? *Shto joker?*' What is joker? The fairy could fly in the air, but she knew neither Hindi nor English.

But laughter is the same in any language. She looked so comically puzzled, repeating the word 'joker', that Rajoo could not help laughing aloud. That made her laugh, too. And then this laughing duet continued for several minutes though neither of them knew why the other was laughing!

Rajoo remembered Mary telling him—how many years ago was it?—'Remember, our first meeting has auspiciously begun with laughter ...'

And now this second meeting, too, had begun with a hearty laugh. Or was it the same first meeting?

Only the names had changed. Mary had become Marina, their forms had changed, the brunette had become a blonde, but the reality was the same. Or was it?

5

Kalooram, the cashier of the circus, too, was a clown in his own right. Midget-sized, loose-fitting clothes, steel-rimmed spectacles balanced on a hawk-like nose. He did not walk, he bounced. He did not talk but gesticulated. But still no one ever made fun of him, for he was the giver of their daily bread—or the money to buy bread! Whether one needed an 'advance' or an increment in his salary, whether one wanted a few days' leave or a job for one of his relatives or friends, it was to Kalooram that one invariably turned. Today it was from his hands that the Russians were getting their pocket money in advance.

Kalooram was assiduously pronouncing—or mispronouncing—the Russian names in a register. 'Mister Ivanov—Mister Moskovsky—Mister Kokakolof—' and each of the Russians was saying 'Da—da' and taking the envelope meant for each one of them.

One of them opened the envelope, saw the two hundred-rupee notes and exclaimed with joy, 'Ah—*dengi!*' Oh, money!

Kalooram, however, did not know that '*dengi*' in Russian meant 'money', and when he silently expressed his ignorance of what was being said, the

Russian said, 'Rupee—rupee!' Only then did Kalooram realize that they were thanking him for the pocket money that he had advanced to them. But he looked at his register and found one name unaccounted for. So he asked them, 'Has your ringmaster saheb come? There is money for him, too.'

'*Shto? Shto?*' the Russian asked, not understanding what Kalooram had said.

'Not stove, I am talking about your ringmaster,' said Kalooram in exasperation and when the Russians shrugged their shoulders, the cashier set off on his own. He had to find the elusive ringmaster as, without making that payment, he could not close his ledger.

Near the lions' cages, Rajoo was still searching for Marina's dog, for it would give him another excuse to meet the Russian beauty. Seeing him standing near the cages, apparently on terms of intimacy with the wild cats, Kalooram decided this must be the lion tamer.

'Good morning, Mister White Man. By any chance, are you the Russian ringmaster?'

'I ... Russian master?' Rajoo repeated with surprise, but Kalooram did not notice the question mark in his tone.

'The moment I saw your blue eyes, I was sure

you must be a Russian!' Kalooram proclaimed, expansively.

'So you, too, have been taken in by these blue eyes of mine?'

Kalooram was gaping with wonder at this Russian who spoke Hindi with such fluency. Then he asked, 'Brother Russian, where did you learn to speak such good Hindi?'

Now Rajoo had to assume the Russian nationality. Since the morning, he had heard Russian spoken and, being such a good mime, he could reproduce the intonation and the accent of any foreign language if he could hear it being spoken only once. Adopting a Russian accent he said, 'I learnt it in Moscow University. My teacher, Professor Shreematikov, used to say that you speak Hindi like the Hindustanis.' Then he spoke some gibberish which sounded, to the untrained ear of Kalooram, like fluent Russian.

'Very glad to meet you, Mister—' he said. 'What is your good name, please?'

'Name? My name?' Rajoo was taken unawares, but he rose to the occasion. 'Rajoo—that is Rajovsky. Ivan Rajovsky. And may I ask your name, Sir?'

'My name is Kalooram. But you may now call me Kalookov Ramoosky.' Then he laughed at his own joke, and Rajoo joined in the laughter.

Kalooram wanted to finish the money transaction so as to call it a day. 'Take this, Sir, with our compliments,' he said, offering an envelope.

Accepting it, Rajoo asked, keeping up the Russian accent, 'What's it? A love letter?'

'More than a love letter.' Kalooram laughed. 'There is money in it—rupees—for your pocket expenses. Understand?'

'Yes, I understand, I understand it too well,' said Rajoo weakly, taking out two hundred-rupee notes but Kalooram was already walking away.

Rajoo was looking fascinatedly at the hundred-rupee notes—he had not seen so much money at one time in several months. Now he could pay the arrears of rent, he would call a doctor to see his mother, buy medicines and milk and fruit for her.

But, meanwhile, he saw Kalooram returning with a giant of a man, and his heart sank at the thought of possible detection. He took care to shove the money into his pocket before the two came up to him.

'Mr Sher Singh,' said Kalooram, pointing to Rajoo, 'Meet your Russian counterpart—Mr Ivan Rajovsky. Mahender Saheb tells me he will perform with your lions tonight.'

Rajoo was unnerved to hear about the lions, and gave a furtive backward glance at the ferocious beasts growling in their cages. But he did not allow his nervousness to become apparent, even when Sher Singh took his hand in his powerful wrestler's grip. He bowed to the Indian ringmaster and let loose a string of Russian-sounding gibberish.

Kalooram proudly informed Sher Singh, 'Mr Rajovsky—he can speak our Hindi, too, very fluently.'

Sher Singh said ominously, 'He may speak Hindi but does he understand the language of my lions?'

'That I understand too well,' answered Rajoo, adding a few impassioned expletives in his pseudo-Russian. Then he calmly said in Hindi, 'But, Mr Sher Singh, you better prepare your lions for the performance tonight.'

Then he bowed stiffly, raised his hat in a gesture of farewell, and walked away, holding his chest out, but the heart within was quivering with fright.

'Russian ringmaster!' spat out Sher Singh in anger and contempt, and then, eyeing his lions, he said, 'Just watch how I prepare them!'

A stable boy was wheeling a trolley with pieces of meat and bones for the lions. 'Bhiku!' barked out Sher Singh, and the man stopped and looked back, waiting for orders.

'Let the lions miss a meal, Bhiku,' ordered Sher

Singh with a vicious glint in his eyes. 'I want them to be hungry for their performance tonight.'

6

The night (according to the announcement made by Mahender) was a memorable one, for it was for the first time that the Soviet and Indian circus artistes were performing together.

Mahender came riding on a white horse. Marina came in a glittering palanquin carried by six uniformed bearers. She was presented to the audience by Mahender. 'Miss Marina, the most beautiful and talented trapeze artiste of the Soviet Union.' The spectators greeted her with thunderous applause.

Marina! Once again a bell rang in Rajoo's mind as, dressed in the ringmaster's uniform, he stood waiting in the wings. Mary–Marina! Marina–Mary!

But now Marina had hauled herself to the top of the trapeze platform where Mahender was already waiting for her. Both of them excelled themselves in that joint trapeze act, but Rajoo kept staring up only at Marina. How beautiful she looked as she seemed to float in the air, swinging from one trapeze to the other. Like a fairy flying without wings! Watching her, Rajoo forgot the dangerous game he would have to play when he entered the enclosure for his act with the lions. (He had already taken the precaution of passing on the two hundred rupees to an Indian clown to deliver them to his mother—in case something untoward happened to him!)

After Marina and Mahender came Seredov, the Soviet Union's most popular circus clown. This was the same Russian (Rajoo smiled as he remembered the misadventure of that morning) who was almost thrown out by the Pathan watchman. First Rajoo was mistaken for Seredov, then Seredov was mistaken for Rajoo! Wasn't it a huge joke? Indian joker. Russian joker. How many jokers? Rajoo carefully watched the performance of the Russian clown. Every limb of his body was attuned to the music; he walked, tripped, got up, bowed, danced, pranced, musically but comically, throwing the spectators into fits of laughter. All this, Rajoo thought, he would have to learn if only he remained in the circus, and remained alive after that night's encounter with the lions!

Then he heard Mahender's voice over the loudspeakers: 'Ladies and gentlemen, we now present Soviet Union's fearless lion-tamer, the great Ivan Rajovsky!'

The circus arena resounded with applause. But inside the dressing tents, where the Soviet artistes were sitting ready for their acts, there was confusion and consternation. For they knew that because his plane had been delayed due to snowfall in Moscow, their ringmaster had not yet come with his bears. In any case his name was not Ivan Rajovsky. Who was this impostor who was claiming to be a Soviet lion-tamer?

Rajoo, alias Ivan Rajovsky, in red velvet ringmaster's uniform, presented an impressive figure as he entered the enclosure. A tremendous applause broke out as he greeted the audience by stiffly bowing and then raising his right hand which carried a whip. From a distance, he looked really formidable. But if someone had seen him at close quarters, one would have found the pallor of fear on his face, and his legs shaking in velvet breeches and embroidered long boots. He maintained the pose of fearlessness so long as the enclosure was empty. But he could not keep up the bold front once the doors of the cages went up and, one after the other, the lions started jumping out and taking up their menacing positions on the stools assigned to them. Rajoo would greet each new arrival with a wave of his hand and a comical grimace as if to say, 'Brother Lion, I am no lion-tamer, no ringmaster, I am a fraud, an impostor, really a joker. Don't attack me with those claws. I am your friend.'

But the people roared with laughter, for they took it to be a new act, a rare combination of a ringmaster and a clown. They took Rajoo's gestures of fright to be simulated fear, for no ordinary joker would venture into the arena of the lions! Indeed, Rajoo's friendly overtures had evoked a corresponding response from the lions. They were happy that the new ringmaster was prepared to leave them alone; he neither whipped them, nor brandished a revolver, nor did he attack them with an iron chair held like a weapon in his hand. Today he was not even cracking his whip to humiliate them by making them run in circles!

While the spectators were enjoying this variation of the ringmaster's routine with the lions, there was grim disappointment on the face of Sher Singh who was standing in a dark corner, near the main switch. He had expected the hungry lions to tear the Russian ringmaster to bits—at least to frighten him out of his wits and out of the lion's enclosure! But this one was surely a magician, for he seemed to have mesmerized the ferociously hungry lions into submissive cats. At that moment his eyes focused on the switch, and a fearful decision was made in his mind. Tired of waiting on their stools and anxious to go back to their cages where they hoped to get a meal at last, the lions had begun to growl. The 'Russian' ringmaster was fearfully walking backwards, when Sher Singh switched off the current and plunged the arena in total darkness.

Just then the manager of the Russian group, through the interpreter, was explaining to Mahender that some impostor was masquerading as a Russian lion-tamer. When the lights were switched off, Mahender's first thought was for the safety of that fraud. Whoever he was, in the dark, the lions would maul him to death. Groping his way, he ran towards the enclosure from where was heard the roar of the lions and the fearful shrieks of the man who claimed to be Ivan Rajovsky. Marina had also come out and was now telling Mahender in Russian, 'Please, please, do something to save this man's life!' Mahender had to shout, 'Sher Singh! Sher Singh!'

By now it had been revealed to Sher Singh that this was no Russian lion-tamer but an Indian who had undertaken the suicidal masquerade for the sake of two-hundred rupees. Contrite and anxious, he switched on the lights, and jumped into the enclosure. The panicky spectators saw the lions running all over the enclosure, the ringmaster nowhere to be seen. For a minute, Sher Singh, facing the beasts, wondered if the hungry lions had devoured him with all his clothes!

Sher Singh took no time to send the unruly lions back into their cages. After all, he had trained them and they obeyed his commands. When the last one of them was safely back in his cage, there was general applause for his courage and resourcefulness, which Sher Singh duly acknowledged. Just then a child pointed, and everyone looked up in that direction to see a funny sight. The one who was supposed to be the Russian ringmaster was dangling from the top of a rope ladder, and making clowning gestures from that dangerous perch. Once again the people laughed and clapped for this brave and brilliant clown who, a few moments ago, had faced a whole pack of lions. It was a three-cornered tableau. The spectators were laughing, clapping, whistling, and laughing again. Rajoo, dangling from the rope ladder, was mimicking a clown. Now he would wave his hand, saying, 'Ta-ta, ta-ta,' again he would wave his leg, yet again he would join his hands, in the hope that he would be forgiven. But the one man who was not likely to forgive him was Sher Singh, who was pointing a fist at him, as if saying, 'You fool, you just wait till I lay my hands on you!'

7

It was a strange court martial. In the office tent of Mahender, the Soviet artistes sat on one side of a long table, the Indians on the other. Between them were seated Mahender himself and the head of the Soviet group, assisted by the interpreter. Across the table, like a prisoner in the dock, stood Rajoo.

Among the Soviet artistes, Marina, who had encountered Rajoo in connection with her dog, was looking intently at the shabbily dressed young man and wondering what had prompted or provoked him to enact the dangerous game with the lions. Rajoo, too, looked at Marina and, with a silent, slight nod, tried to communicate to her how grateful he felt for her sympathetic look. Surrounded by so many apparently hostile strangers, he was greatly encouraged by the flicker of her smile.

Like a judge in court, Mahender addressed Rajoo with cold objectivity, without anger or sarcasm or bitterness. 'You speak the Indian language, you look like a Russian—you are fair-complexioned, with brown hair and blue eyes—and your dress is a hybrid combination. Who *are* you? What *are* you?'

Rajoo answered, 'Is it not sufficient for you that I am a human being, and that, like all humans, I possess two eyes, two ears, one nose, one stomach—and one heart! You call me Rajoo, or you may call me Rajovsky. But I am I, and …' He raised his right hand at the characteristic gesture that was his trademark. '… *mera naam* Joker!' And then with a strange, sad smile he asked, 'Is it really necessary to put a label on this empty bottle?'

Mahender, impressed and moved by the argument, now asked, 'Never mind about your identification. Tell us what made you impersonate the Russian lion-tamer? Why did you tell such a big lie?'

Rajoo looked across the length of the table, directly into Mahender's eyes. 'Shall I really reveal the secret?' And he glanced at the long line of Soviet artistes.

'Yes, do tell us,' replied Mahender. 'They are our friends and colleagues.'

'Then listen, please,' Rajoo started speaking. 'Because small lies are no longer a paying proposition. This is the age of the big lie. Women who use the big lie of cosmetics are called beauty queens; those who tell big lies to hoodwink the public are called leaders and politicians; and in the world of business, the bigger the big lie, the more black money in the bank vaults!' Then that mysterious and sad little smile reappeared. 'I am only a small operator in this big business of the big lies!'

Mahender was so moved by this statement that for a few minutes he did not speak. Meanwhile, the interpreter translated Rajoo's words for the benefit of the Russian artistes, and they nodded sympathetically. Then Mahender said in a tone that was stern and yet concerned, 'But it did not occur to you that this Big Lie could have cost you your life?'

Sher Singh, who was seated next to Rajoo, added in a powerful booming voice, 'The lions could have devoured you in no time. Were you not afraid of that?'

Rajoo looked sheepishly at the mountainous ringmaster. 'I must admit I was afraid. But there is one thing that is even more fearful and ferocious than the lion.' Then he addressed them all: 'And that is poverty and hunger. I needed money at any cost—not only to feed myself and my mother, but to get medicine for her. My mother has been ill for a long time. I had no money to take her to a doctor. I tried everywhere for a job but got nothing but refusals. No one wants to employ a joker, a man who only knows how to laugh and to make others laugh. If that is all you know, they taunted me, try your luck in a circus. And the fact is that, for truth, even the doors of the circus were closed. So, to get in, I had to take the help of such a big lie.'

All the artistes seated around that table, Indians and Russians, were visibly moved by Rajoo's pathetic tale of woe. Tears glistened in the beautiful brown eyes of Marina.

But Mahender was matter of fact as he said to his colleagues, like a judge asking for the opinion of the jury, 'Well, comrades, what punishment do you suggest for the prisoner at the bar?'

There was whispering among the Indians and the Russians, then the verdict of each side was whispered to Mahender. The verdict, delivered dramatically by an artiste who was also a showman, was pronounced in a grave, sympathetic tone.

'Rajoo alias Ivan Rajovsky! You have been found guilty of the crime of common humanity. Therefore, this court sentences you to an indefinite detention in this circus—till such time that you, yourself, choose to be free!'

Only then did Mahender permit himself a friendly smile, as he joined the others in applauding the judgement. Marina was the most enthusiastic of all and, as she clapped and clapped, she got up from her seat. The clown Seredov embraced Rajoo in the Russian fashion, and kissed him on both the cheeks. Sher Singh lifted him up in his powerful arms. Then everyone saw that tears filled Rajoo's eyes—tears of relief, of gratitude, of happiness—and his lips were trembling as he tried to express his thanks. The lips continued to tremble and quiver but he could utter not one word. Whatever he felt, whatever he wanted to say, was silently conveyed by his tearful eyes.

8

Rehabilitated in the circus community, Rajoo was walking out of Mahender's tent when he saw someone in the moonlight, waiting for him. For a moment he missed a heartbeat. Could it be as it seemed, Mary? A phantom out of his past? Or was it Marina? Were his eyes playing tricks in that emotion-charged moment?

When he went nearer, he saw that it was Marina—she must be waiting there for someone else. Perhaps for Mahender Saheb or for one of her Russian colleagues. They were not even introduced, so there was no question of her waiting for him. He walked on but then he was stopped by a sweet, soft voice.

'Rajovsky—*Tovarisch* Rajovsky!'

Rajoo turned round. It was Marina and she was indeed calling him. Near her stood the interpreter Rybakov.

Rajoo took off his hat to greet the lady.

Marina answered with a smile.

He went near her and smiled.

Finding him smiling, she smiled again.

Then Marina said something in Russian, and the interpreter translated, 'Miss Marina says you are a very strange man.'

'Thank you,' said Rajoo and, lifting Marina's hand in his own, he kissed it, as he had seen the Russians doing among themselves. Then he uttered the single Russian word that he had learnt, 'Spassiba.' Thanks!

Marina looked surprised, and said something in Russian.

'She wants to know why you are thanking her.'

'Because at least she regards me as a human being even if it is a strange one!'

When it was interpreted in Russian, she said something with a look of concern.

'She says that when you were with the lions, she was greatly worried about your safety.'

Before Rajoo could say anything, the interpreter was called away by someone else, and he apologized and left.

Now Rajoo was left alone with Marina.

Now that he was seeing her all alone, Rajoo's senses started playing tricks with him. Not only his eyes. He could smell the perfume that he had carried with him on Mary's wedding day.

Then he convinced himself that it was not Mary. It was Marina. He spoke, slowly, articulating each word separately, 'You—were—concerned—for—my—life.' In pantomime gestures that accompanied the words, he pointed to her, then he pointed to himself and his heart, and then he assumed a look of concern.

Marina nodded and said, 'Da-da!'

Rajoo asked, 'Da-da? That means yes-yes?'

Marina, now in a playful mood, imitated him, 'Yes-yes? Da-da!'

'And what is Russian for no-no?' He shook his head and repeated, 'No-no?'

Marina understood him and said, 'Nyet-nyet—no-no.'

'Nyet-nyet.' Rajoo imitated her. 'No-no.'

'No-no. Nyet-nyet!' Marina repeated the lesson.

Now it was two little children repeating the lessons in school.

'Da-da—yes-yes!'

'Yes-yes—da-da!'

'Nyet-nyet—no-no.'

'No-no—nyet-nyet.'

From a distance, a Russian girl's voice called, 'Marina! Marina!' Then the voice said something in Russian. Perhaps they were calling her—it was time to go. Marina pantomimed to say that she had to go.

'Nyet-nyet. No-no,' pleaded Rajoo.

'Da-da. Yes-yes,' said Marina. Then, smiling and waving her hand in farewell, she went away, and while going, said, '*Dosvidaniya.*'

'Now what does that mean,' wondered Rajoo.

Meanwhile, he saw the interpreter, Rybakov, returning that way, and he promptly buttonholed him. 'Just a minute, Mister. Tell me something.'

Rybakov answered in his slow and bookish Hindi, '*Kahaiye—kya kathinai hai*?' Tell me—what seems to be your difficulty?

Rajoo asked, 'What does *das-bi-daniya* mean?'

'Not *das-bi-daniya* but *dosvidaniya*—it means we shall meet again.' Then the interpreter, who was in a hurry, was gone, saying, '*Dosvidaniya!*'

A broad grin appeared on Rajoo's face. Again and again he repeated the word, like a magic mantra, '*Dosvidaniya!* We shall meet again! *Dosvidaniya!*'

We shall meet again. Who shall meet again? Rajoo and Marina? Or Rajoo and Mary?

'*Dosvidaniya!*' It was not a word in Russian but the refrain from the song of his destiny. 'We shall meet again!'

Then he went home, muttering the Russian phrases he had learnt that day.

'*Dosvidaniya*—we shall meet again!'

'Da-da—yes-yes.'

'Nyet-nyet—no-no.'

'Da-da—yes-yes.'

'Yes-yes—da-da.'

After years, he felt a positive, hopeful emotion in his life.

'Da-da—yes-yes.'

Next day when Rajoo entered his room, his mother was pleasantly surprised to see him loaded with all kinds of vegetables, lentils, cooking oil, and a week's rations. From his pockets he extracted bottles of mixtures and packets of tablets for his mother. But all the time he was speaking some mysterious mantra.

'Da-da—yes-yes.'

'Da-da—*dosvidaniya.*'

She was surprised at all the things her son had brought, but what pleased her most was his happy mood.

'What is it, Son? You look very happy today?'

'Da-da!' The son replied.

'Have you got a job?'

'Da-da!'

'What is all this da-da-na-na?'

'No, no, Ma, no na-na, only da-da. Now everything will be da-da. It means yes-yes.'

'Is that true?'

'Yes, Ma. Whatever you say, da-da. It will be done.'

'All right. Then bring me a daughter-in-law.'

'Oh, a daughter-in-law?'

'Now say da-da!'

'Ma, God willing, that too will be da-da one day.' Then he got up from her bed to put away the medicine bottles in the cupboard.

'A million thanks to you, Bhagwan,' the mother prayed to the Almighty. 'My Rajoo has at last got a good job. Now, if only he would bring a daughter-in-law, this house would be filled with happiness.'

Meanwhile, Rajoo was looking at that little joker in its hiding place in the cupboard, and talked to it in whispers to avoid his mother hearing him.

'Baba, give me your blessings, for like you, I too have found my destiny and my destination in the circus!'

Hearing his mother's footsteps, he quickly closed the cupboard and turned round to meet his mother's complaint.

'You haven't told me what kind of a job you have got.'

'Ma!' Rajoo hesitated to tell an outright lie. What he said was true and not true. 'A job is a job, Ma. You know it means a lot of work. But this is a rather strange kind of business—it is work, as well as pleasure!'

'Business? Is it some kind of shop?'

'Yes, yes, Ma. You may call it a store—you find everything under the sun. All right, Ma. I'm getting late. I'll be going now. Will come home rather late.'

'What kind of a shop is this, my son, that opens both in the day and at night?'

Rajoo had to quickly find the answer. 'It's just like the chemists' shops. You know the day-and-night dispensaries which keep open at all hours. Goodbye, Ma. Don't forget to take your medicine.'

He made good his escape, otherwise he was afraid the truth might come out in the course of her relentless cross-examination.

He could not afford to displease his mother—nor could he afford to miss this chance.

The same circus, which his mother associated with death, was the only glimmer of life, of hope, that he had seen in a long, long time.

9

When Rajoo reported for his first day's work, Mahender handed over to him a long-handled broom.

'Take this.'

Rajoo accepted it but with some hesitation and misgivings. He had expected that he would be asked to perform as a clown; he was hoping to match his wits with the Russian Seredov, and instead he was being asked to sweep the circus arena!

Mahender read Rajoo's unspoken thoughts and doubts and said, 'As you become a member of the circus fraternity, this will be your first job—to sweep the floor, to use this broom to clean the refuse from the stables, to wash the lions' cages, and to give a bath to the elephants—they can't live without water. You know why I'm entrusting this menial work to you?'

'No, Sir.'

'Because you can't fly—either in the air or from one trapeze to another—without first planting your feet firmly on the ground. Twenty years ago, when I was a boy, that's how I began my life in the circus.'

Finding Rajoo reacting with astonishment and disbelief, Mahender added, 'If you want to rise in the world, you must begin at the bottom of the ladder.'

And now he—he who owned the circus, and was its most important performing artiste—extended his powerful hand towards the sweeper with the broom. Rajoo experienced the grip on which depended Mahender's own life and the life of his partner—Marina—while performing the most intricate and dangerous acrobatics on the flying trapeze. Through Mahender's extended hand, Rajoo felt the softness and warmth of friendship.

'Thank you, thank you, Sir,' said Rajoo, and Mahender left him to himself. Now he was alone with his broom.

He had just cleaned up the elephants' stables when he met the Russian clown, Seredov, who was going to do a rehearsal of some of his acts.

Rajoo recognized him and said, '*Namaste*.'

Seredov greeted him in Russian, '*Zdrastvitya*.'

Rajoo, while shaking hands, echoed his greeting, fumbling a little, '*Zad-draast-viti-ya*.'

Rajoo smiled.

Seredov grinned.

Rajoo grinned.

Seredov took off his hat.

Rajoo took off his hat.

Seredov bowed.

Rajoo bowed.

Seredov pointed to a step-ladder which was one of his props.

Rajoo pointed to the broom which was his only prop.

Joker!

Joker!

Russian joker!

Indian joker!

How many jokers were there, really?

Rajoo resumed his sweeping, but to his functional movements of clearing the dirt was now added the posture and the rhythmic gestures of a clown.

Seredov placed the rim of his bowler hat on his nose and, surprisingly enough, it stood there, while he moved about to maintain the balance.

Watching him with professional interest, Rajoo put away the broom and tried to balance his own battered felt hat on his nose. But it collapsed at the very first attempt.

Then Seredov handed to Rajoo his own stiff bowler hat, and pointed to Rajoo's nose. Soon Rajoo found out the trick. Inside the hat there was a dent, shaped to fit the bridge of the nose, and that was how the stiff bowler hat could stand, balanced on the nose.

Now that he knew the trick, Rajoo too could balance the hat on his nose, and climb the step-ladder, deliberately missing some steps to appear clumsy to raise a laugh.

'*Kharasho! Ochin Kharasho!*' Good! Very good! Seredov exclaimed with delight, translating the exclamation into the only Hindustani words he knew: '*Achcha! Bohat achcha!*'

When Rajoo climbed down, took off the hat and bowed, Seredov applauded. Then he proceeded to embrace his Indian pupil and rival, and kissed him on the cheeks.

Not to be outdone, Rajoo too kissed Seredov on the cheek.

Neither was prepared to admit defeat, and they continued to peck at each other's cheeks for a long time.

To vary the gesture of friendship, they shook hands warmly.

Then Seredov said in Russian, 'You are a born clown, my friend,' and Rajoo who didn't know the meaning of the Russian words, still understood what Seredov was trying to convey.

As he merrily swept the floor of the empty circus ring where the different artistes were rehearsing, his actions were noticed by Mahender and Marina from their lofty perch on the trapeze platform. Mahender pointed to the sweeper below.

'You see that fellow Rajoo?'

'Rajoo?' Marina was not yet familiar with the name. 'Oh, Rajovsky?'

'Yes, one day he will become a great joker, you understand?'

Marina shook her pretty head, for she did not understand.

'Joker—that is clown. You know *clown*.'

Marina repeated the Russian pronunciation of that word, '*Klon!* Oh, *Klon! Da-da!*'

'He is a born joker,' Mahender said while looking down at Rajoo. 'When he is in trouble, he laughs. When he should weep, he sings ...'

Rajoo was singing as he swept the dirt and the dust, the animal refuse and the filth of the circus stables. This was a comic song that he had composed himself out of his own experiences. On the road of life, he had been repeatedly pushed about, and hefty men had kicked him around, many recklessly driven cars had all but knocked him down. Also he had seen many arrogant ones stumble and fall. His song was a warning to all of them—the careless, the reckless, the haughty and the arrogant, with the lilting refrain—'Watch your step, my friend, watch out!'

As he went around the circus, sweeping with his broom, and watching the men, the women, and the animals at work, he kept on improvising additional stanzas, but always coming back to the refrain—'Watch your step, my friend, watch out!'

Lustily repeating this musical refrain, he ran into Mahender, who caught him by the neck.

'Was it you singing while at work?'

'No, Sir—I mean yes, Sir—' Rajoo was taken aback, confused and flustered, pleading with his boss, 'I promise you, Sir, I'll never do it again.'

Mahender shouted at him, 'You'll have to do it again. You'll do it every day!' And then he put away his angry mask and smiled, 'From today you are a clown—the Singing Clown. Understand?'

Rajoo couldn't believe his ears. 'Yes, Sir—you mean in this circus?'

'Yes, in this circus and in no other.'

'Thank you very much, Sir, Mahender Saheb.'

'My name is neither sir nor saheb. It is only Mahender.'

'Yes, Sir, Mahender Saheb!'

'Not saheb, but Mahender.'

'Yes, Mahender—Saheb!'

Mahender laughed aloud at what had become a gag. 'You are incorrigible.' Then, seeing Marina who had just come out of her dressing tent, Mahender pointed to Rajoo and said, 'He is going to be a joker—a clown! The Singing Clown.' Then he was gone, but Marina chose to linger.

'Hello,' she said at last.

'Hello.' Rajoo looked at Marina.

'*Zdrastvitiya,*' she said. '*Na-mas-tay!*'

'*Namaste,*' Rajoo responded. '*Zad-drast-ti-vi-tiya.*'

Rajoo took off his hat and brought out a red rose from inside it.

Marina asked in Russian, pointing first to the rose and then to herself, 'Is this for me?'

'Da-da—yes-yes.' Rajoo replied, repeating last evening's Russian lesson. He wanted to say, 'I gave such a red rose to Mary—and today I am offering it to you.'

Accepting the flower, Marina said, '*Kraseeva*—beautiful!'

Rajoo pointed to her and said, 'You, too, are *kraseeva!*'

Marina said, '*Spassiba.* Thank you. *Dosvidaniya.*' And with a friendly smile, she was on her way.

'*Das-vi-da-niya!*' Rajoo repeated the farewell greeting, translating for his satisfaction—'We shall meet again!'

When he was alone, he spoke to himself, 'So you are a joker at last—a joker who will sing—and make people sing. Just like your father! Are you destined to meet with the same end?'

10

That night, in the presence of five thousand spectators packed in the circus—and in the presence of Marina who was watching from the wings—'Rajoo the Singing Clown' was born.

That night, and on subsequent nights, along with the performance of the Russian artistes, Rajoo sang his satirical songs, and the people laughed heartily at his jokes; they laughed till they could feel their sides splitting. But they knew that this was no ordinary clown, he was different from all the clowns they had ever seen before. Hidden within him they glimpsed a man who had graduated from the school of life, who had walked along the dusty paths, seen his country and met his people, laughed with them, suffered with them, walked with them, talked to them, seen them labour, and suffered with them all the privations and deprivations to which they were heir. Here was a man who had tasted love and suffering at an early age, and had assimilated it all. All these feelings and facets of life, but above all compassion and fellow-feeling, were in his songs and in his clowning. He made people laugh because he himself had learnt to regard life as the supreme joker.

He was not just a joker with a painted face and a funny costume who made people laugh by his comical appearance. In his art, his humour, his jokes, his clowning, he showed the mirror of life to people. They saw such absurd faces and figures that they invariably burst out laughing, but while laughing they began to suspect that probably these ridiculous faces he had shown them in his mirror were reflections of their own features. And they laughed all the more because they felt, and they knew, that they were laughing at themselves, at their own follies and foibles.

Marina's feminine intuition told her that Rajoo, when he was not clowning, was silently watching her perform on the trapeze. In those blue eyes—blue like the deep blue ocean—she sensed peace and happiness. They encouraged her, inspired her, emboldened her to perform with greater skill and daring. Then, when her act was over, with the applause still ringing in her ears, she would climb down from the trapeze and find him standing in the wings. He greeted her with a smile, and brought out a red rose from the inside of his hat and presented it to her.

Then it happened that, when he was performing, he saw from the corner of his eye that she was watching him with joy and with pride, and then Rajoo would be performing not for five thousand people but for just an audience of one, to make one girl laugh, and when she did at last burst out laughing at his clowning, he felt immeasurably rewarded, supremely fulfilled.

One evening, when Rajoo finished his performance, there was tremendous applause, and he noticed that Marina too was enthusiastically clapping.

While still clapping, she spoke to him, 'Bravo, Rajoo, *ochin kharasho*.' He had learnt enough Russian to know that she was saying, 'Well done, Rajoo. Very good.'

Rajoo said, '*Spassiba*', and lifted her hand to plant a kiss on it—Russian style.

He said, '*Shukriya*', and kissed it again.

Then he said, '*Dhanyawad*', and repeated the kiss.

Finally, he said, 'Thank you, Marina', and was kissing her hand, to her amusement and obvious pleasure, when Mahender observed this drama and laughingly asked, 'Rajoo, how many languages do you know?' Then he told Marina, 'Come on. They are all waiting. It's our turn.'

Marina pointed up to the trapeze and said in Russian, 'I have to go.'

Rajoo countered it with 'Nyet-nyet. No-no.'

Marina laughed. 'Da-da. Yes-yes.'

Rajoo insisted, 'Nyet-nyet!'

Marina said, '*Dosvidaniya*' and translated it for him, 'We shall meet again!' Then she took Mahender's hand and together they went to the arena.

A big applause greeted them and, as he watched her climbing the rope ladder, Rajoo wondered, 'Is it Marina? Or is it Mary? And if she is not Mary, why does my heart beat faster whenever I see her? Is it not true that you love only once in your life?'

11

Ringmaster Sher Singh was known as Ustad or Guru by the whole circus community. He trained them in wrestling, helped them to build up their muscles, and taught them all the tricks of the trade. Whenever anyone had any problem, one approached the veteran Sher Singh for advice.

One day, while he was relaxing in front of his tent, he saw Rajoo coming towards him in a thoughtful mood.

'Ustad!' said Rajoo.

'Hoon!' Sher Singh belched and then said, 'You seem to have some problem on your mind.'

'It's a very big problem, Ustad. But I feel shy to tell you.'

'A circus man, and that too a joker, should not feel shy,' Sher Singh guffawed loudly. 'Only when a man is free from all inhibitions is he able to make people laugh. Sit down and tell me all about your little problem.'

Rajoo sat on the edge of the chair and asked, 'May I ask you something?'

'Yes, yes, go on. Have no fear.'

'Ustad, have you—ever loved someone?'

Sher Singh laughed outright. It was like the roar of a lion. 'First you tell me, Rajoo. Have you ever wrestled with a lion?'

'I tried once,' confessed Rajoo, remembering his encounter with the lions, 'and had to beat a hasty retreat. You had to come and save me.'

Now the veteran heaved a long, deep sigh. 'You know, once I, too, loved and had to beat a hasty retreat.'

'A brave man like you?' Rajoo exclaimed in surprise. 'You, a tamer of lions?'

'Listen, Son. Between ten hungry lions and one beautiful girl—do you know who is more dangerous?'

'I'm beginning to catch on a little, Ustad-ji. The one who's more beautiful is the more dangerous one.'

Rajoo (Rishi Kapoor) and David (Manoj Kumar)

Vidyadhar Kamat (Kamat Foto Flash)

Marie (Simi Garewal)
and Rajoo (Rishi Kapoor)

Vidyadhar Kamat (Kamat Foto Flash)

Rajoo (Rishi Kapoor) plying his wares

Vidyadhar Kamat (Kamat Foto Flash)

Rajoo (Raj Kapoor), Kumar (Rajendra Kumar) and Meena (Padmini)

Vidyadhar Kamat (Kamat Foto Flash)

Vidyadhar Kamat (Kamat Foto Flash)

Marina (Kseniya Ryabinkina), Mahender (Dharmendra) and Rajoo (Raj Kapoor)

Vidyadhar Kamat (Kamat Foto Flash)

'Right, absolutely right. Remember, this game of love is very dangerous. Beware of your limbs—and your heart!'

'Ustad-ji,' Rajoo assured him, 'I'll be able to look after my limbs, but I am not so sure of my heart.'

'Then may God protect you.'

'*Dosvidaniya*, Ustad-ji.'

'What's that? What language is that?' the ringmaster asked, surprised to hear the strange word.

'It's Russian for goodbye,' said Rajoo. 'I am trying to learn a little Russian with the help of this dictionary.' And he took out a Hindi–Russian conversational guide.

'So!' The ringmaster winked as he chuckled. 'And is it true that someone else is trying to learn Hindustani?'

Rajoo came away, thinking of what the veteran Sher Singh had said.

Beautiful! Fearful! Dangerous!

What is beautiful in Russian? *Kraseeva.* Da-Da. *Kraseeva*!

And fearful? Dangerous? Nyet-nyet. No-no. He will not look up such words in the dictionary.

12

Approaching Marina's tent, Rajoo put the Hindi-Russian dictionary back in his pocket, and cautiously peeped inside.

Marina was seated in front of her dressing table, teaching herself to talk in Hindustani with the help of the Russian-Hindi dictionary.

'*Kak vi Pozhivaetay*,' she read from the book. '*Aap kaisay hain*—How are you?'

'*Ya kharasho*,' Rajoo whispered in reply. '*Main achcha hoon*—I am all right!'

But loudly he said, '*Mozhna*.' It was just one Russian word but (according to the dictionary) it contained a whole sentence. 'May I come in?' And the funny thing was that to say 'Yes, you may come in', Marina too would have to repeat the same word.

But Marina did not say '*Mozhna*'. She surprised Rajoo by uttering with only a slight trace of accent, '*Haan, haan, aaiye*.'

When Rajoo had gone in, Marina got up to greet him and joined her hands, Indian style. '*Namaste*,' she said.

Rajoo countered with '*Zdrastvitiya*'. How are you?

Marina promptly began, '*Aap—aap—*' and then

she flipped the pages of the book, and added, '*Aap kaisay hain*?'

Rajoo, too, now had to take out the little book from his pocket and, after consulting it, he said, '*Kak vi pozhivaetay*?' How do you do?

Now that the secret of their proficiency in Hindi and Russian was revealed, they both laughed out aloud, holding their precious little books.

Rajoo said, 'Now you can speak Hindustani fluently and, with the help of this dictionary, translate it into Russian.'

Marina replied with some effort, '*Aap—bhi—Roosi—bohat—boltay—hain!*' You, too, talk too much Russian. She had meant to say that he too spoke Russian well.

But Rajoo laughed at her delightful mistake and said, 'That's the whole trouble with me—I talk too much!'

Again the two laughed.

Rajoo offered her a parcel wrapped in tissue paper, and they talked in a mixture of basic Hindi and basic Russian.

'Is this for me?' Marina asked.

'Yes, please open it and see.'

Marina opened the packet and took out a white silk sari. '*Ochin Kraseeva!*' she exclaimed. 'It's very beautiful!'

Rajoo, with the help of pantomime gestures, suggested that she should try it on.

Marina had seen Indian women wear saris, but didn't know how they were worn. She tried to wrap the sari around her, over her mini frock, and in the process presenting some amusing variations. It became, by turns, a Roman toga, a Southeast Asian sarong, a Punjabi lungi, a Rajasthani ghoongat, and a Muslim burqa. But whatever way she draped the sari, to Rajoo she looked exquisitely beautiful. She was delighted with her experimentation, as she watched herself in the mirror, and Rajoo watched her, fascinated. As if he had never before seen a beautiful girl wearing a sari!

In a way, it was true. Mary always wore a frock, dress, or skirt and blouse. The schoolboy Rajoo often thought of presenting a sari to Mary and requesting her, for his sake, to wear it once and then visit his mother. But in those days he had neither money to buy a sari, nor courage to say anything to Mary which she might resent as too presumptuous on his part. Today he had bought and presented the sari to Marina. But could he tell her to come with him to see his mother?

At last Marina successfully draped the sari in a more-or-less proper style. When she put the palloo over her head, she looked like a shy Indian bride!

With difficulty she spoke the Hindi words: '*Main—kaisi—hoon?*' How am I? She meant: How do I look?

Rajoo awakened from his reverie. 'Perfect. You look very beautiful. If my mother could see you as you are, it would make her very happy.'

'Ma!' Marina articulated the word as if it were a beautiful and sacred but strange word for her, which she had never uttered.

'Yes—Ma! You know what is Ma. Mummy. Mother. Mama,' Rajoo explained.

Marina said with great feeling, 'Nyet Mama. Papa!' No mother, only father! And she looked at a middle-aged man's photograph on the dressing table.

Then she asked in Russian, 'Where is Mama?'

'Will you come and meet my mother, Marina?'

'Da-da. Yes-yes. I will be happy to meet your mother.'

Rajoo felt immeasurably happy as he said, 'And my mother will be overjoyed to meet the fairy of her dreams!'

13

The chawl where Rajoo lived with his mother was in the slums of Bombay, but it seemed the whole of India lived there.

In his neighbourhood resided people of all regions, and all religions—Hindus, Muslims, Christians; Maharashtrians, Gujaratis, Punjabis, Poorbis, south Indians, Sindhis, Goanese. A dozen different languages were spoken within the rooms of this building. But the language they spoke to each other, on the staircases, the corridors and the balconies, wherever they happened to meet each other, had no printed dictionary. It was a hybrid but colourful language through which millions in the city conversed with each other, and which could be called 'Bombay Hindustani'.

When Rajoo brought Marina to this chawl, the whole neighbourhood curiously watched Rajoo with a fair, blonde girl, obviously a foreigner, though dressed in a white silk sari. Here was an event that would give the idlers something to talk about for days.

The mother lay ill on her cot. When the door swung open on creaky hinges, she opened her eyes. Rajoo was entering with some girl whom she could not see clearly because they were silhouetted against the light streaming in through the open door.

'Ma, here is the fairy of your dreams,' said Rajoo; but he spoke in Hindustani, and Marina thought it was just an ordinary introduction.

The mother was sick and weak, but when she heard this, she tried to sit up.

Marina joined her hands and said, '*Namaste*.' Then she sat down on the edge of the bed.

His mother looked at her visitor.

Marina looked at Rajoo's mother.

The mother thought, 'So this is what a fairy looks like in human form.'

Marina thought, 'Here before me is the mother I've never known.'

The mother's arms were now extended to receive her, and Marina felt drawn towards them. The next moment the mother was clasping the girl to her bosom. In the old woman's imagination, the shehnai began to play. Affectionately caressing the girl, she uttered the conventional words of blessing. 'May you live long, Daughter. May you be blessed with marital happiness. May you have sons and grandsons!'

Marina could not understand the colloquial language in which the blessings were worded, and she enquiringly looked at Rajoo who told her, with the help of the dictionary, that the mother was blessing her.

Marina gratefully looked at the mother. '*Spassiba*, Mama. Thank you.'

The mother now looked askance, first at Marina, then at Rajoo. What language was she speaking?

'Ma, Marina does not speak our language,' Rajoo explained. 'She is not an Indian.'

'Is she a Bengali, then?'

Rajoo shook his head.

The mother looked appraisingly at the girl. 'Her skin is very fair. She must be from Kashmir.'

Rajoo quickly said, 'Yes, yes, Ma, she comes from a country not far from Kashmir,' and then fearing his mother should say something tactless that would give the game away, he hustled Marina to her feet.

'Ma, you rest now. We have to go back to work. She has a job in the same company where I work.'

The mother gestured to Rajoo to come near her, then whispered, 'Whoever she is, I like her. But aren't you ashamed to make her work for a living?'

'Don't you worry, Mother,' Rajoo reassured her. 'I am thinking on the same lines.'

While bidding goodbye, the mother again embraced Marina. 'Daughter, I am entrusting my Rajoo to your care. Look after him. He is very sensitive—any unkindness breaks his heart.'

Marina asked Rajoo, 'What did Mama say?'

Rajoo stopped near the cupboard. A thought had just occurred to him. 'Ma said that no guest who comes in the first time should be sent back empty handed. She wants me to give you a present.'

He opened the cupboard and took out the little joker to give it to Marina.

'What is this?' she asked, holding up the doll.

'*Eto ya*,' he said in Russian. 'This is me. Keep it with you.'

Marina looked at Rajoo. His eyes were full of hope and love, nervousness and happiness—and, overcoming them all, a silent question.

Marina held the little joker next to her heart, and this was her silent answer to the silent question he had asked.

14

The little joker, duly installed in a place of honour on Marina's dressing table, stared at her with his blue glass eyes. Whenever she looked down to pick up something, she found the little one ogling at her.

'Mischievous fellow!' she said in Russian. 'Staring like that! Have you never seen a girl before?' Then she picked it up, held it upside down, tickled it, then clasped it to her bosom, and gently kissed it.

Just then, from outside, came Rajoo's voice. 'May I come in?' And then to show off his knowledge in Russian, he asked, '*Mozhna?*'

Marina quickly replaced the little joker and

prepared to receive its bigger counterpart. 'Da-da. *Pazhalasta.*' Please come in!

Both first did 'namaste' to each other, then said '*Zdrastritiya*', then bowed to each other, then they both laughed, and only then did Rajoo remove his hat and bring out a red rose to offer to Marina. Marina tenderly kissed the rose and kept it carefully near the little joker.

Rajoo was fumbling for words to say something profound and important, and laboriously consulted the dictionary for that purpose, when Rybakov, the interpreter, burst into the tent. He seemed both happy and excited. He said something to Marina in Russian, on hearing which she danced with joy. Rajoo, feeling left out of the happy occasion, had to ask, 'What is it, Rybakov?'

Rybakov switched over to Hindustani. 'The circus is going on tour. We will see all the famous cities of India. Won't it be wonderful?'

'So the circus is going on tour?' Rajoo repeated without enthusiasm.

'Yes,' said the interpreter, 'you, too, will sure come with us?'

'But who will look after my mother?'

Marina anxiously asked, 'What about Mama? How is she?'

How was Rajoo to explain to her the dilemma that confronted him? If he left Bombay, he would have to leave his sick mother behind. If he did not go, it would be a separation from Marina which, too, he could not bear.

So he said, 'Nothing, nothing at all,' and, by force of will, removed the signs of worry from his face. Laughing, he told Marina, 'Now, Marina, I will show you my country.'

Marina asked in her halting Hindustani, 'Have—you—seen—the whole—of—Hindustan?'

'Yes,' replied Rajoo, mimicking her speech, 'I—have—seen the whole—of—Hindustan! You—know—I am—a—born—vagabond! *Awara hoon.*' Then he translated it into Russian, '*Ya Bradyaga!*'

She smiled and clapped her hands at the prospect of seeing India.

'It will be even more wonderful now,' he added, 'because I will see it through your eyes.'

From Bombay to Nagpur—Nagpur to Madras—Bangalore ... From city to city, the circus toured the country, and the Indian and Soviet artistes performed together. For the Indians it was routine—they had gone round the country several times—but for the

Soviet artistes, it was an opportunity to view the great and fascinating cities of India.

Rajoo had seen it all, but through Marina's eyes it looked different and wonderful—the old and the new, the architectural marvels, the symbols of progress and new life. Rajoo showed her not only the India that the tourists see but the real India, not only the big and palatial hotels but also the little homes and huts and hovels, and the little men and women who lived there and who all seemed to know Rajoo and welcomed him like a member of their family. They were happy to receive his Russian friend, too, and treated her with great kindness. One particular family of a working man in Mysore lavished such hospitality and affection on her that Marina felt deeply moved. They gave her coffee in little brass cups, served piping hot snacks straight from the frying pan, and the schoolgoing daughters entertained her with songs and one even danced for her. When she took leave of them, there were tears in Marina's eyes. The housewife said to her, 'Come again, Sister. But please excuse us, for our house is very small.'

Marina answered, and did so in Hindustani, '*Ghar—chhota—dil—bada.*' Small house, big heart! Hearing it, the sturdy working woman beamed with happiness, and embraced the delicate Russian beauty.

Marina saw India through the eyes of Rajoo, and as she came to know the country and the people, the culture and their simple way of life, her fondness for Rajoo grew. On his part, Rajoo was wrapped up thinking of Marina—of new ways to amuse her and entertain her, to watch the wonder in her eyes as she reacted to some architectural monument or some exquisite spectacle. There were twenty other Soviet artistes, men and women, and Rajoo had made friends with several of them. But he saw only one face, heard only one voice—Marina's. These were the happiest days of his life.

They found happiness just to be in each other's company. They would begin to laugh like little children, for no apparent reason. They overcame the problem of communication by learning a few key words of the other's language. But they usually didn't need to speak. A look, a gesture, the merest touch was enough to express what they felt for each other. Now they treated each other with affectionate informality.

One night, Rajoo had satirized a very fat and muscular strongman. As he parodied the weightlifting feats with a gutta-percha baby doll, the audience had laughed its guts out. Marina was still laughing as she called Rajoo into her dressing tent.

'Rajoo, today you were great—you excelled yourself.'

Rajoo, who was wearing the cotton-padded 'body', showed off the exaggerated muscles, and parodied the swagger of the strongman. 'See these muscles—feel them—hard like stones, eh?'

Marina kept up the joke, took out her camera to photograph him with his 'body beautiful'.

Rajoo posed.

She clicked her camera.

Rajoo laughed.

Marina laughed.

They both laughed.

While laughing, they came very close to each other.

Then Marina said in Russian, '*Ya loobloo vas, Raj-joo.*' I love you, Raj-joo! She had an endearing way of pronouncing his name with the accent on the second syllable.

Rajoo replied in Hindustani, 'Marina, I too …' Then his courage failed him. What seemed shameless and presumptuous in his own language could be uttered only in his halting Russian. So he said, 'I too *loobloo* you!'

They were already so near that Marina had just to pout her lips to kiss him.

As she did so, the whole strength seemed to drain out of his body—actually, the pumped-in air in the artificially bloated 'body' leaked out with a hissing sound.

Sher Singh entered the tent hurriedly and was not amused by the spectacle of the deflated strongman. He held a telegram in his hand, and his expression showed that he was the bearer of bad news.

'What has happened, Ustad?'

Sher Singh replied, 'Bad news from your home. Your mother is seriously ill. Mahender Saheb says you should be immediately sent back by plane.'

15

Sitting by the sickbed of his mother, Rajoo remembered the happy days spent in the company of Marina and felt guilty.

Was God angry with him for deserting his mother and leaving her to be looked after by their neighbours? It was true that in Marina's company he forgot everything—including the sickness of his mother. This was probably the sin for which he was being punished. Could loving be a sin? He had heard that one realized God through love. Then why was he being tortured and punished?

He silently prayed to God. 'Let my mother recover from this illness. Let her be well. I promise that I will never leave her again, not even to go to the circus.'

Where would the circus be now? Delhi, Agra, Lucknow? The Indian and Soviet artistes would be entering the arena in a procession, seated on elephants, waving colourful flags and banners. The spectators must be applauding the entry of Marina as she came riding in a palanquin, resplendant in her gorgeous, sequined white dress. His friend, the Russian clown Seredov, in baggy pants and patched-up coat, must be walking in, wiggling his hips, to the delight of the children. Mahender and Marina must be performing miracles on the trapeze. The fairy must be flying through the air. Marina! Would she be missing him? Another worry. Would the spectators be missing him?

Whether it was the beneficial effect of the doctor's medicines or of the prayers of the son, or of his devoted care, Rajoo's mother slowly recovered. Now she could sit up in bed, reclining against pillows.

One day the son said, 'Ma, Doctor Saheb says now you are out of danger and will recover soon.'

The mother replied in a weak but firm voice, 'It's not the doctor I need. What I need is to see my daughter-in-law once again. What's her sweet name?'

'Marina.'

'Very beautiful. She is, indeed, a fairy,' she said with such love that it seemed to illuminate her face. 'My heart yearns to see her.'

'Ma, once you get well,' the son reassured her, 'you can see her as many times as you wish. But first you get well. Only then will I bring her to see you.'

The mother smiled softly. Rajoo, too, forced himself to smile. He knew it was a false hope he was giving her, because in a few days the circus was returning to Bombay, when the Soviet artistes would give their farewell performances. And then it would be time for them to leave. The fairy would fly away, to the land across the snow-covered Himalayas. Then what explanation would he give to his poor, innocent mother?

16

When the circus returned to Bombay, Marina was overjoyed to see Rajoo. She hugged him and kissed him, and told him in gushing Russian that she missed him everywhere, that without him nothing was the same. Then she translated in her halting Hindustani. 'Calcutta—Delhi—Lucknow—Agra—*magar achcha naheen—laga?*' She did not enjoy any place.

'But why?'

'Because you were not there.'

'Is that true, Marina?'

'Da-da?' Marina nodded.

'Nyet-nyet!' Rajoo shook his head.

Both laughed at their old joke, but there was a brooding shadow over their laughter. They were both trying to forget the imminent parting.

'*Kak* Mama?' Marina asked. How's Mother?

'She is better now, but remembers you all the time.'

'Then come, let's go to Mama.' She caught Rajoo's hand and tried to drag him, and he had to restrain her.

'Marina,' he said, and deliberately used Hindustani words, as a screen to cover the unpleasant reality, '*Main tum ko kaisay samjhaoon ke Ma tumhen apni honaywali bahoo samajhti hain?*'

She could understand only a few words: '*Main*' was 'I', '*tum*' was 'you', 'Ma' was 'Mama', but what was '*bahoo*'? That, she felt, was the key word.

'What is *bahoo?*'

To evade a direct answer, he spoke in elaborate and colloquial Hindustani. 'In every mother's heart there are two compartments. In one lives her son. The other is vacant for her *bahoo*.'

'*Naheen samjhi!*' I don't understand! She was worried by what she did not understand.

'It is very difficult to make you understand. It's better that you understand it only when you go back to Moscow.' Then he got up to go. 'I will just go and see Mahender Saheb.'

After Rajoo abruptly left, Marina kept worrying about his behaviour. Why didn't he want her to go with him to see his mother? What did the word '*bahoo*' mean? She hoped it did not mean something bad. She kept repeating the word, rolling it over her tongue. '*Bahoo? Bahoo?*' Then she suddenly thought of consulting the dictionary. Taking up the little book, she turned over the pages. '*Bahoo*? ... *Bahoo*! ... Daughter-in-law. The wife of the son!'

The colour drained out of her cheeks. So Rajoo's mother wanted to make her the wife of her son. She wished with all her heart it could be possible! But she remembered her crippled father—his leg had to be amputated after it had been hit by a bullet during the war—who was waiting for her return, just as Rajoo's mother depended on her son. Apart from her father, there were only two persons whom she had learnt to love—Rajoo and his mother—and now she would have to cause pain to both of them. She had not known any mother except Rajoo's mother. In her she had found the warmth, the sweetness, the softness of mother's love. And now she would go away, breaking that loving heart. 'What shall I do? What can I do?' The question kept haunting her till she saw the little joker that Rajoo had given her, saying, '*Eto ya*'. It is me! Then she knew what she had to do.

17

That evening the whole of India—that is Rajoo's entire neighbourhood—saw that the same foreign-looking, fair-complexioned girl who had come once before, was climbing the rickety staircase. Today she was alone and she was not wearing a sari. The frock that she wore came barely above her knees. 'One of those memsahebs,' the elders decided, reluctantly looking away from her bare legs. 'But why is she going alone to see Rajoo's mother?'

There was a timid knock on the door, and Rajoo's mother called out from her sickbed, 'Come in.' The door opened and she was deliriously happy to see Marina entering. Was she dreaming or was it the same fairy whom she had mistaken to be a Bengali beauty, and then a flower from Kashmir?

Joining her hands, Marina said, '*Namaste. Aap kaisi hain?*' How are you, Mama?

Making her sit by her side on the bed, the mother said, 'Only today I was telling my Rajoo to bring you home. Now you will see how quickly I will recover!'

Marina could not bear to look at her loving face. Averting her eyes, she said in Hindustani, 'Mama, Rajoo—is—very—good …' and then she could not carry on, and lapsed into Russian, 'I have seen only one mother—and that is you—so much love I have received from you, I cannot tell you how I value it. You are the last person I want to cause any pain. I don't want to hurt Rajoo either. But, Mama, what am I to do? I have to go back to Moscow tomorrow, where my crippled father is waiting—he has no one else to look after him—I have to go, I have to go, Mama …' And she burst into tears.

The mother did not understand anything of what Marina had said, except the name of Rajoo and the word 'Mama'. She clasped the weeping girl against her heart, and said, 'Daughter, don't cry. Is it that you are remembering your mother? I will be a mother to you, I will give you all my love. Only once you settle down in this house!'

Marina also did not understand what the mother was saying. 'No, no, Mama. I am talking of Rajoo.'

'Rajoo!' The mother misunderstood her reference to her son. 'Has Rajoo said or done anything that has made you cry? Let him come. I'll take him to task. I'll give him such a thrashing that he will remember all his life. He has no business to be rude to my darling fairy.'

The mother had used the Hindustani word 'pari' which Marina understood. So she said, 'Mama, I am not the fairy of your dreams; I am a simple Russian who has to go back tomorrow to her country, to her old and crippled father. I am helpless, Mama, I am helpless.'

Then she remembered a few Hindustani words. '*Mera dil ro raha hai.*' My heart is crying. But this was all she could say. Then she lapsed into Russian again. 'Now I have to go. It is time for our farewell performance. *Dosvidaniya*, Mama!' Then she left something wrapped in paper on the bed and ran away from there.

The next moment the whole of India—the entire neighbourhood of Rajoo—saw that a girl, in a frock that barely came down to her knees, was sobbing, tears flowing down her cheeks, as she came down the stairs. They all exchanged knowing glances which were not devoid of compassion. These foreign 'memsahebs', too, were after all human creatures!

After Marina was gone, the mother picked up the packet and was surprised to find the little joker wrapped up in it. How did Marina come to have it? She wondered and then thought, 'Surely, Rajoo must have given it to her.' But before she could wonder why Marina had returned it, the mother saw the circus poster in which the doll had been wrapped. On the poster, on one side was her fairy in the trapeze costume and on the other her Rajoo dressed up as a clown—laughing and making others laugh—just like his father who, too, used to be on every circus poster!

18

That night there was an unusually big crowd to watch the farewell programme of the Soviet circus artistes.

The Pathan watchman escorted an old woman wrapped up in a shawl to Sher Singh. 'Saheb, this lady has no ticket, but she insists on going in.'

The woman who was not only old but looked ill and worried now said, 'Let me in, Son. My Rajoo works here in the circus. I have come to watch his performance.'

'Oh, so you are the mother of our Rajoo. Please come with me,' said Sher Singh. Then he dismissed the watchman, saying he would personally see the old lady to her seat.

On the way, Sher Singh casually remarked to cheer up the old lady: 'Mataji, your son is a remarkable clown. He does incredible things to make people laugh.'

The widow remembered her husband who also used to do the most incredible things to make people laugh, and spoke as if she had heard of an impending catastrophe. 'Does incredible things to make people laugh? That's what I am afraid of, Son!'

The show began. Amidst general applause appeared Mahender and Marina and bowed all round to the audience. Then Mahender started climbing the rope ladder to the trapeze platform. Now it was Marina's turn. Rajoo's mother saw her fairy smiling, but it was a mechanical smile behind which were lurking tears.

Rajoo came as Marina climbed up to the protective net. Wearing the clown's make-up, with a straw hat on his head, he looked just the replica of his father. Would he meet the same end? His mother shuddered when she saw that Rajoo was trying to climb up to the giddy heights to deliver a red rose to the fairy. Marina climbed the rope ladder expertly, easily, but Rajoo simulated fear, hesitation, clumsy and perilous footholds as he went up to the net, and tried to walk over it, stumbling and falling. This was a special act devised by Rajoo for that occasion, and Marina had to simulate coquetry, beckoning him, but managing to keep herself beyond his reach. Rajoo did not have to pretend to be the ardent wooer who would undertake any risk to deliver the flower to his lady-love as he inexpertly, clumsily, negotiated the rope ladder, holding the flower clenched between his teeth, and swung perilously, sending the spectators into peals of hilarious laughter, and causing his nervous mother to miss a heartbeat.

Finally, Rajoo the joker managed to climb up to the trapeze platform, but just as he offered the rose to Marina, she swung away from that platform, caught another swinging trapeze midway, and swung herself to the opposite platform. Now Rajoo was left standing on the high platform, with a gaping chasm between him and Marina—who was smilingly beckoning him to her side! (They had rehearsed this act together several times, but today it had a peculiarly symbolic poignance.) Rajoo answered in pantomime gestures that he was scared of that dangerous distance, that he couldn't swing that far. His comical gestures were broad enough to be observed by the audience below but they laughed at the apparent humour of a clumsy and cowardly joker stranded in space and unable to propel himself on the trapeze to reach the beauty inviting him at the other end. But the irony of these gestures was beyond them. It was a secret between Rajoo and Marina, and the only person who could guess it was the mother. She was watching the dangerous game with apprehension in her eyes, and gently praying to God to protect her Rajoo.

The fairy who could fly in the air, who could swim through space, was inviting the joker to cross over the deep chasm, but the joker could not fly in the air to take the leap into the dangerous unknown. He was scared, his legs were trembling, as he stood on the stage of what was certain doom—looking helplessly across the distance at the beckoning fairy. But love triumphed over fear, and the joker, too, caught hold of the trapeze and propelled himself into space.

He almost reached across; the fairy extended her delicate hand to support him; he came near enough to deliver the rose—his message and symbol of love—but not near enough to catch the fairy's hand. Every time he swung, there was an increasing distance between their hands that were trying to reach out to each other. The joker was desperately trying, and comically failing, to reduce this distance, and the spectators were laughing. This act of 'the Joker, the

Fairy and the Red Rose' was the most entertaining hit of the evening's performance.

The joker swung in space like a human pendulum, trying to reach out to Marina at one end and to Mahender on the other platform. He seemed to be scared, was actually screaming. (This was all part of the act. The joker is never scared, but only pretends fear, for he represents the weak and the timid.) But the mother was choked with terror. 'Oh God, is the tragedy of twenty years ago to repeat itself?'

Rajoo, in trying to catch the other trapeze, let go of the one he was holding on to. Now he was coming down, waving about his arms in a comical simulation of panic. The mother's heart, watching the son's fall as if in slow motion, frantically leaped up to save her son, and was still for ever.

Rajoo fell on the taut net that was stretched for just that purpose.

He fell and he bounced up.

The people laughed, the people applauded.

Rajoo fell again and bounced again.

The spectators continued to applaud. This joker was really marvellous, always conjuring up unpredictable new gags.

Finally, when Rajoo bounced, he stood up on his two feet firmly planted on the elastic net. In this moment he saw, and recognized, his mother seated there in the front row, looking at him with a fixed stare, as if silently accusing him, 'Son, you didn't heed my warning!'

Rajoo, forgetting his role as a performer and a clown, addressed an audience of one, his mother.

'Ma! Now you know the awful but inexorable truth. I lied when I told you that I was working as a salesman in a shop. But, if you ask me, this work in the circus, too, is a salesman's job. We sell happiness and joy, and in return buy pain and sorrow for ourselves.' He did not know what a great sorrow he was buying at that poignant moment. Then he told her what he had wanted to tell her all along. 'Ma! What else could I do? Where else could I go? The blood of my father was singing in my veins, *Jeena yahaan, marna yahaan ...*'

He could not complete the refrain of his father's song, for he saw someone touch his mother and her body roll over. It seemed as if she was already dead. Suddenly he realized that she had been staring at him with lifeless eyes ...

He cried out in anguish, but he could articulate only one word, the first word that a child learns to utter after birth, the last word that he utters in every crisis of his life: 'Ma!'

19

The backyard where the residential tents of the circus personnel are lined up, along with the cages of the animals, the wagons and other miscellaneous props, are always full of life and the noises associated with life. One can hear the roar of lions, the trumpeting of elephants, the laughter of children, the chatter and gossip of women. But when Rajoo rushed there, he encountered only the solemn silence of death. Before he saw his mother, he had a premonition of her death.

Men and women stood with their heads bowed down with grief. But it might be that they had misunderstood her state. She might have been rendered unconscious because of the shock. Rajoo rushed to her side and, sitting down, he saw the deathly pallor of the face, felt the hands and feet that were cold and lifeless. The fact of death was now confirmed. But Rajoo did not cry out, no tears flowed from his eyes. But something snapped within him. He knew now that the days of his youth were over. So long as she was alive, he had always regarded himself as a boy. He had laughed and cried, and been obstinate and mischievous, he had lied to her and stolen things from her—and all this he was able to do because he had a mother to coddle him and pamper him. He had nothing and yet he had everything—the boundless love of his mother. However worried and dispirited he came home, the understanding, indulgent smile of his mother revived his drooping spirits. There was a rare communion between the mother and the son. For Rajoo, she was everything—father, mother, brother, sister, friend. He had no one else in life. He was still a child when his father had passed away; he remembered him only as a faint childhood memory. But the enduring memory of childhood was the sweet and comforting presence of his mother. How beautiful she looked then! But gradually, the rigours of being a widow, of prolonged illness and the grind of daily toil had taken their toll. Her complexion had darkened, her features were criss-crossed with wrinkles. But today, in death, the lines of age and pain had magically vanished. Once again she looked as beautiful as were Rajoo's childhood memories of her. Was it because, having died, she had at last been freed forever from all the pain, all the illnesses, all the torturous realities of life?

Rajoo felt the soft pressure of someone's hand on his shoulder. He looked up at the kind and sorrowful face of Mahender. That touch and that look of compassion brought tears to his eyes.

A bell sounded somewhere in the backyard of Rajoo's consciousness. It seemed far and distant, and totally irrelevant, till someone shouted, 'Rajoo, the time for your act!'

Rajoo heard it, looked at Mahender as if to say, 'How is it possible, Mahender Saheb? Can a man perform to make people laugh immediately after the death of his mother?'

Mahender did not answer his silent question in his eyes. He only turned to one of his assistants and ordered, 'Give me the mike.'

When the microphone was handed to him, Rajoo expected to hear Mahender say that he regretted to announce that due to the sad demise of his mother, Rajoo would not be able to perform that night. But, instead, he heard Mahender say (and his voice boomed through the loudspeakers and echoed with the applause from the circus), 'Ladies and gentlemen, now we are proud to present to you India's greatest, the most unique, and the bravest joker—Rajoo!'

Rajoo's eyes were now overflowing with tears; still he was fixedly staring at Mahender, questioning him, 'What kind of a grim joke is this, Mahender Saheb? Is this a test of some sort? Don't you think I am human?'

Mahender, reading the silent questions in the tear-filled eyes of Rajoo, helped him to his feet and, looking him straight in the eye, said, 'Rajoo, my friend, today the world will know at last how great the heart of a joker is!'

Rajoo kept on shaking his head to say, 'No, no. I can't perform tonight.' Then he turned and quickly went away towards his dressing tent.

Mahender had covered the dead body with a shawl when Sher Singh handed over to him the little joker which someone had brought. 'This was lying on the seat where Rajoo's mother was sitting.'

Mahender took the little joker and for a long time continued to look at the doll-face of the joker whose destiny is to laugh and to make others laugh, even though his own heart might be breaking!

20

People remember that night as legendary. They saw Rajoo giving a memorable performance. He sang and he danced, and he mimicked and he clowned as he had never done before. He made the people roll with laughter, while his own heart was breaking. At the end he sang a song that summed up his mood, the moment, and the clown's eternal philosophy:

This world, this, indeed, is a circus.
And the circus is a show of three hours.
The first hour is childhood.
The second hour is youth.
The third hour is old age.
And then? And then, my friend?
There is no father and no mother.
No brother and no sister,
No beloved and no lover,
Neither this nor that—
Nothing whatsoever remains—
No sign or symbol of life.

Hearing that song, tears came to the eyes of those who knew of the death of Rajoo's mother.

There were tears in the eyes of the matter-of-fact Mahender.

Sher Singh, the lion-hearted, was crying like a child.

The ever-jovial Russian clown, Seredov, who was always laughing and making people laugh, was sobbing.

In the beautiful eyes of Marina, there were not only tears but there was a great pain, sorrow and regret. She wished she could be the fairy of the dead woman's dreams, and do something to console and comfort the bereaved Rajoo.

Rajoo's song spoke of great emptiness, the great silence and solitude that come in the wake of death, in terms of the 'three-hour show' of the circus:

> Nothing remains,
> No sign or symbol of life—
> Except the rows of empty chairs
> Except the desolate ring—
> The forsaken nest of a bird
> Who has flown away for ever!

When the words failed him, and his voice trailed into a wailing, Rajoo took out a little violin and drew from it a melancholy melody that was like a lost soul crying out in the wilderness. It seemed that the joker's violin was crying out because it was forbidden for the joker to cry ...

Now, in fact, the circus arena lay empty, shorn of the morning light, row upon row of unoccupied stairs.

The show was over, the spectators had gone home.

The Big Top that, not long ago, was full of life and laughter, now lay deserted, desolate, dead!

Only the sound of the canvas tent flapping in the morning breeze was heard.

And, wearing again his old clothes in which one

day he had entered the circus, his haversack slung on his shoulder, Rajoo passed through the desolation, ready to take to the road.

21

Mahender sat in his office tent, waiting for Rajoo. He had a premonition that last night was Rajoo's last performance, that he would leave the circus for ever. But he knew that, before going, he would come to bid him goodbye.

He saw him coming in, ready for departure, and his worst fears were confirmed.

'Mahender Saheb, the show is over. Now I am going.'

'Rajoo, my friend, my brother, don't go away. Stay with me.'

'Mahender Saheb, no one can stay with anyone forever. Even my mother couldn't stay with me.' There were tears in his eyes. Then, after a pause he said, 'You had punished me for the common crime of humanity. I hope I have served out my sentence. Now, I take your leave.'

'But where will you go?'

'This wide world itself is a circus. Somewhere, somehow, I will get a chance to perform.'

'But something tells me that one day you will return to us.'

'That I promise you. Before I die, I will come back to your circus to give the farewell performance of my life.'

Mahender took out a pair of dark glasses and slid them across the table. 'Accept this as a parting gift from me.'

'What shall I do with it?'

'Wear it.'

'Why?'

'Because you are a joker and no one should see tears in a joker's eyes.'

Rajoo put on the dark glasses, though tears continued to trickle down his cheeks. He got up.

'Let me take my leave now, Saheb.'

'How many times have I told you that my name is not Saheb but only Mahender.'

'Yes, Mahender—Saheb!'

He left and, while going, made Mahender laugh with his old, old gag.

22

Marina was coming through the deserted circus arena when she spotted what she was seeking—Rajoo standing in a corner, against the background of circus posters with his laughing face. Going near him, she noticed the dark glasses he was wearing.

'Rajoo!' she said with great tenderness, 'you are crying?'

'Mother has left me forever. Now you are going away.'

Marina said something in Russian which was incomprehensible to Rajoo.

'*Ya ni punnimayoo!*' At least he could tell her in Russian that he did not understand.

'*Naheen samjhay?*' She fell back on her fragmentary knowledge of Hindustani. 'I am saying *dosvidaniya.* Till we meet again! If we don't part, how shall we meet again?'

'I am not a philosopher,' mused Rajoo bitterly.

'Every joker, every clown, is a philosopher; has to be a philosopher,' Marina said with great conviction. 'Look at me, Rajoo. I love you. My heart is crying at the thought of parting. Still I am smiling. We meet to part, we part to meet again. That is life.'

'If that is life, what is death?'

'That, dear heart, I do not know.'

There was a pause. Then Marina asked, 'Rajoo, are you angry?'

Rajoo shook his head to say—no.

'Are you sad?'

Rajoo shook his head again.

'Then take off your dark glasses.'

Rajoo took off the dark glasses slowly. There were no tears. The eyes that emerged from behind them were smiling, though in their depths, there was infinite sadness.

23

The Soviet circus artistes were being garlanded by their Indian counterparts before the departure of the plane to Moscow. There were warm embraces, cordial handshakes, words of farewell. Mahender was bidding goodbye to the head of the Soviet group. Seredov, the Russian clown, was embracing the same Pathan watchman who had nearly turned him out of the circus on the very first day. But Marina's eyes were searching for Rajoo whom, at last, she found among the other circus artistes behind the airport railing. As before, his travel kit was on his shoulder, ready for a lonely journey.

Marina ran up to him, impulsively embraced him. Their lips met in a long and lingering kiss.

The Russian artistes were already beginning to board the plane.

Rajoo pointed to the plane, the flying palanquin, which would take away his fairy to a distant fairyland.

Marina had a lot to say, but she did not know how to say it in Hindustani. So she spoke in Russian.

'Rajoo, will you sing for me the song from the film *Awara*? From the time that I was a little schoolgirl, I have loved this song. It always speaks to me of India. Now it will speak to me of you.'

Once again, they embraced, once again their lips met in a kiss, but this time it was shortened by the emergency of departure. Forcing back her tears, she ran to board the airliner.

Sher Singh, the rugged ringmaster, standing by Rajoo's side, asked him, 'We heard, or rather saw, what she said to you in the language of love. But, while going, what is it that she said to you in Russian?'

Rajoo simply said, 'She reminded me of an old, old song.'

As the huge plane began to taxi across the runway, Rajoo's song was heard, telling of a tramp who was ever on the move, but ever hopeful, ever optimistic.

The plane was now zooming into the sky. Marina, sitting by the window, was watching Rajoo getting farther and farther away, though he was standing still at the airport. It was *she* who was going away!

And now, his bag on his shoulder, he was walking again on the road of life.

On Rajoo's lips was the song of the eternal tramp.

In his heart were memories of Mary, and of Marina.

In his haversack, among other necessities of life, was the little joker, his one constant companion, ever reminding him of his destiny.

Part Three

FEVER OF SUCCESS

1

Now he walked alone. He had no father, no mother, no friends, no neighbours. But the world was his home, and his heart was open to all strangers. Every man was his friend, his comrade, his neighbour.

The passing years deepened the lines on his face. The pain and the sorrows of life were reflected in the depth of his deep blue eyes. But that little joker—the symbol of his destiny, the one constant companion of his boyhood and his youth—continued to have the same innocent smile frozen on his face, looking at the world with eyes full of amusement. It seemed as if he had discovered the great secret that life was a huge joke, a game of alternating light and darkness, day and night, happiness and sorrow. Who was playing this game—and why? Even the wise ones had not been able to find an answer. But if it was a joke rooted in eternity, there must be a Supreme Joker who was laughing at the absurdities, the oddities, the frivolities, the follies, and the foibles of life.

Rajoo continued to move from place to place. But despite his endless wanderings, he didn't seem to get anywhere. He was like a rat in a trap, wandering, running, capering within the confines of his imprisonment. It was a journey without any progression. He had started from Bombay and eventually found himself again in that city. Last time, he had a home of sorts. This time, he had no home. The endless footpaths with their beds of stones invited him every night, but he preferred to sleep on the velvet softness of the sands, to the soothing music of the sea waves.

But one day he sat on the beach, tired and exhausted by the struggle for existence. It was not only that he had no job and no money in his pocket, but that he had not eaten for two days. A great and wise man, a saint, had said that to a hungry man even God must appear in the form of bread. Rajoo now realized that a hungry joker is a gloomy joker. Laughter itself had been starved to death. What, then, is the purpose of life? Why make all this exhausting effort for survival if it was to lead to the nothingness of an empty stomach? The sea was cool and deep, and enticingly inviting. Why not take the easy way out?

He took the little joker out of his haversack. There was the same hilarity on its face, as if it were laughing at him, making fun of him, ridiculing him for admitting defeat so easily.

'So easily?' thought Rajoo bitterly. 'I will teach you a lesson. I will drown you first, before I end my life.' With whatever strength remained in him, he threw the clown–doll, it made an arc, and plummeted down into the sea. Rajoo hoped he had got rid of the little mischief-maker. But on his face was the expression of a man who had committed suicide.

From behind him, suddenly, came the sound of a dog barking, and Rajoo turned to see a little mongrel racing over the sand. Soon he plunged into the waves, and was swimming towards the little joker bobbing up and down in the water. The next moment, the dog had caught hold of the doll between his teeth and was swimming back to the shore and to him. The doll was wet as it lay at Rajoo's feet, but it had the same laughing face, as if proclaiming, 'You can't kill a joker so easily!'

The dog, a hungry looking creature, was wet but proudly wagging his tail, and seemed to yelp a warning to Rajoo not to do such a thing again.

Stroking the wet fur on his back, Rajoo said to the dog, 'My dear fellow, why did you have to save me from drowning?'

The dog looked with a puzzled expression, and raised a paw to point to the doll that was soaked in salt water, as if to say, 'I only brought out this doll, or it would have drowned!'

Rajoo looked at the dog and spoke in the language of silence. 'This is not just a toy, my friend, *it is me!* A plaything kicked around by destiny, which no one loves, no one wants. Neither Mary, nor Marina, no one accepted me, no one owned me. I wanted to die quietly, but you came in with your Boy Scout tricks. You deserve punishment, my foolish friend!' But already the moment of despair, of fatalistic inertia, had passed. And it was the gay, old joker who threw a piece of driftwood into the sea.

The dog immediately jumped into the waves, and swam to retrieve it.

The joker within Rajoo was now awakened and felt amused. Addressing the dog, he said, 'Smart work. You should have been a police officer.'

Then he used the same piece of wood to draw a big circle on the sand. The dog, yelping merrily, started going round it.

'Bravo, my friend!' Rajoo, whose humour had returned, was clapping his hands admiringly. 'How well you go round and round, yelping the same thing. You ought to have been a politician!'

Now he picked up the little dog and said, 'You are very clever—that is why, like me, you are a homeless wanderer. Will you be my companion?'

The dog shook his head vigorously. The answer was no. Someone, somewhere shouted, 'Moti! Moti!' and the dog jumped out of Rajoo's arms and started running.

Rajoo saw that, on the beach, a big hoarding had been put up, advertising a film called *My Darling*, starring the popular hero, Kumar. On top of a ladder stood a boy, shouting, 'Moti! Moti!' Evidently he had just finished pasting the poster, and was now calling to his dog who, too, was now happily trying to climb up the ladder.

Before the boy came down, he cast a long, lingering look at the famous star, and challenged his giant-sized portrait. 'What do you say, Mr Kumar. One day, my face, too, will be on the posters—and maybe, bigger than yours!'

Walking along, Rajoo had reached the bottom of the scaffolding holding up the poster, and was again trying to make friends with the dog. But soon he had to contend with the owner, for the boy jumped down from the ladder. Rajoo saw this was a beardless youth, dirty and dishevelled, in ragged jeans, worn-out canvas shoes which had holes in them, and an old leather jacket that was too big for him. On his face was a suspicious, hostile look as he advanced towards Rajoo.

'You bloody thief!' hissed the boy. 'You are planning to kidnap my dog!' To Rajoo's considerable surprise, this smooth-cheeked youth of hardly fifteen or sixteen took out a clasp knife, and a sharp blade sprung open menacingly.

Rajoo, the old trouper, was not to be frightened by a mere child of the streets. Still, he took a step backwards, '*Baap re!*' he exclaimed, more amused than angry. 'This boy is a real filmic gangster, ever ready with his dummy knife!'

'Shall I show you how sharp this dummy knife is?' the boy asked and did not wait for an answer, but attacked Rajoo. Had Rajoo not been alert, the blade would have pierced his arm, but luckily he had received training in ju-jitsu from Ustad Sher Singh in the circus and knew how to parry a sudden knife thrust. As the boy lunged forward, he lightly stepped aside and went for the boy's wrist, which he twisted in such a way that the knife flew in the air, and the boy was sprawled on the sand.

Picking up the knife and closing it, Rajoo told the boy, still on the ground and nursing his wrist, 'Children should not play with such dangerous toys. And you imagine I'd run away with your dog?'

The boy nodded.

'But I'm not such a fool as to acquire a hungry dog when I've nothing to eat myself.' And then, turning to the dog, he asked, 'Tell him, Moti, was I kidnapping you?'

The dog shook his head to say 'no'.

The boy, now up on his feet, sullenly told the dog, 'Come on, Moti, let's go.'

'Eh, boy!' Rajoo called after him. 'What's your name?'

'Minoo,' the boy replied, stopping and turning around. 'And what is yours?'

'Rajoo. What do you do?'

Minoo pointed to the scaffolding and the poster. 'Sometimes I get these posters to paste!'

'So!' Rajoo contemptuously looked at the hoarding. 'You make a living by boosting these film stars. And when you don't get this work?'

'Then I do nothing.'

'That means our profession is the same. You do Nothing, I do Nothing.' Rajoo brightened up with an idea. 'Do you know two negatives make one positive? If we combine our two "nothings", the two of us may be able to do "something"—Rajoo and Minoo.'

The dog barked sharply to remind them of his existence.

'And Moti!' said the boy, affectionately looking at his dog. 'But what can we three do?'

'Sonny boy,' shouted Rajoo, extending his hand. 'What can we three *not* do?'

Rajoo and Minoo sealed the pact with a warm handshake, and Moti placed his paw on their hands to remind them it was a tripartite agreement.

2

On a cloth rag, strung like a streamer across the street, was crudely painted 'GREAT INDIAN FOOTPATH CIRCUS'.

A circle of spectators, mostly children, had formed, and in the middle Minoo was beating a drum, Rajoo a brass thali, and Moti, wearing a speckled cloth like a tiger-skin, was saluting, standing on his hind legs. When a sufficient crowd had collected, Rajoo made the announcement in the stentorian tones of an authentic circus barker, but the words had once been uttered by a boy selling eye-powder: '*Hindu ko Ram Ram, Musalman ko salaam, Christaan ko good morning, aur Sardarji ko sat sri-akal.* Friends, Comrades, and Indians.' Then, beating the brass plate again, 'Here is good news, great news, sensational news—the Great Indian Footpath Circus is in your town, in fact it is in your locality, it is right in front of you. Now our famous acrobat, Master Minoo, will bounce like an Indian rubber ball, while executing amazing somersaults.' Turning to Minoo, he commanded, 'Come on, Master Minoo. Show them your amazing feats of skill.'

Minoo literally went head over heels in breathless somersaults, just like circus artistes.

'Well done, Master Minoo,' shouted Rajoo, exhorting an applause. 'Children, do give a hand to Minoo Master.' The kids applauded with gusto.

Minoo acknowledged the applause by making a professional bow which Rajoo, the old circus hand, had taught him. Then it was his turn to make the announcement—and that, too, Rajoo had taught him: 'Ladies and gentlemen, and children, we have the honour to present to you the famous joker of the Great Indian Footpath Circus—Rajoo.'

Rajoo, with a joker's mask on his face, bowed, and then raised his right hand, shouting, '*Mera naam* ...'

The children all cried out in chorus '... Joker! Joker! Joker!'

Now Rajoo did the acrobatics he had learnt in the circus for his clowning acts. Then he announced: 'And now we present a ferocious lion, from the jungles of Africa—the one and only Moti!'

The dog stood up on his hind legs to acknowledge the applause and the laughter of the children.

Minoo held an iron ring in his hands, and at a signal from him, Moti jumped through the hoop, and repeated it several times.

Children laughed, the elders clapped, everyone was happy, everyone was enjoying the show. They were all slum-dwellers, and they had never seen such a hilarious 'circus' before—and this was free!

Now Rajoo was standing on the tightrope, a bamboo stick in his hand to balance himself, and as he started walking on it, his patter continued: 'In the shastras it is written that the path of truth is like the razor's edge. But this long and tight rope is the path of politics. See how our leaders confidently tread the straight and narrow path ...'

As he said this, he slipped and comically fell down, hilariously demonstrating the predicament of the politicians who have a sudden fall!

This time there was tremendous applause, and taking advantage of it, Minoo asked for contribution. 'Ten paisay—five paisay—even your one paisa will be gratefully received.' Coins began to be showered on him, as Rajoo exhorted the children to shout 'Long live the Great Indian Footpath Circus', and Moti went round holding Rajoo's hat between his teeth to receive the coins that people dropped in spontaneously.

3

'Long live …'

'… the Great Indian Footpath Circus.'

Laughingly raising these slogans, they crossed the embankment of the suburban railway line to enter the views of ramshackle hutments. There were big drainage pipes lying about everywhere. Rajoo and Minoo were carrying their 'circus' props on a bamboo pole slung across their shoulders—Minoo in front, because he had to show the way. Rajoo was surprised when Minoo entered a large-sized pipe. Minoo was small, but Rajoo had to duck and bend his head, and he protested as he was dragged into the pipe, 'Eh, Minoo Master, where are you taking me through this gutter?'

Minoo's voice came back in the half light, as they walked through the pipe. 'Don't you dare call this a gutter. This way leads straight to heaven!'

They emerged from the drainage pipe in front of a dilapidated hut that seemed to be lying abandoned.

'This is my heaven!' said Minoo.

Rajoo saw a one-room hut made of bits of wood and bamboo matting with scrap tin sheets on the roofs. 'Your heaven is very—heavenly,' said Rajoo, and then added, 'you must have paid a premium of at least two to three thousand rupees to acquire it.'

'To tell you the truth, I got it free,' replied Minoo, going in through the door and opening the solitary window to admit the dwindling light of the sunset hour. He stood at the window and added, 'The man who built it was run over by a train when crossing over that embankment. Since then people in the neighbourhood say that the hut is haunted by a ghost.'

Rajoo looked back towards the embankment. A train was passing by, with a distinct clatter of the wheels. Then he looked at the darkened house, expecting to see a ghost.

'You mean to say it's really haunted?' he asked nervously.

'That's what people think,' Minoo calmly replied. 'So no one ever comes anywhere near it.'

Rajoo felt reassured enough to enter the hut. It was sparsely furnished—only a *charpai*, a few rags hanging here and there, a pitcher of water in a corner, and an unlighted lantern nailed to the central pillar supporting the roof.

'Minoo, aren't you afraid of ghosts?' he asked, looking around.

Minoo, who was searching for the matchbox to light the lantern, replied, 'Rajoo, I see ghosts even in the daylight. This world is full of them. Why worry about a poor man's ghost?' He proceeded to light the lantern.

In the light, Rajoo could see that it was a big enough room in which two or three persons could easily live together. He said, 'You are right, Minoo, I too am not scared of ghosts.'

Minoo suspiciously asked, 'What do you mean?'

'I mean that I have decided to stay on here,' he said, hanging his bag on the wall, and before Minoo could say anything, he asked, 'How much rent do you pay?'

'Nothing,' answered Minoo, 'but ...'

'So from now on I will pay half of that "nothing".'

Minoo did not appreciate this informality. 'But how will we manage? It's just a little hut. How can we three live here? There's only one cot ...'

'So what?' Rajoo replied. 'I'll sleep here on the ground. Moti can lie down under your cot.'

'And if it gets cold at night?'

'Then both of us will squeeze ourselves under our blanket.'

Minoo flared up. 'Shut up—if you talk such dirty nonsense, I will break your head.'

'All right, my friend,' said Rajoo mock-seriously, apologizing with folded palms. 'You be comfortable on your bed of roses. I am accustomed to sleeping on footpaths.' Then, to change the topic, 'What do you think? Shall we get something to eat?'

But Minoo was more interested in the division of their spoils. 'First let us distribute what we have earned. Take out the money.'

'Yes, indeed, why not?' Rajoo took out the coins which were jingling in his pocket, and counted them. 'In all we got three rupees and forty-three paisay.' And then he divided them equally in three parts. 'One rupee and fifteen paisay for each of us—you, me and Moti.'

Minoo was surprised. 'Will Moti also get a share?'

'Why not?' Rajoo declared. 'Isn't Moti an equal partner in our circus?'

Both of them laughed at this, or rather all three of them, for Moti was also barking to express his happiness.

'Well, Master Minoo, how was our Footpath Circus?'

'Wonderful!'

'Then let's shake hands, Partner.'

Once again when Minoo's fingers came into the grip of Rajoo's calloused hand, he felt something strange about their tapering softness and smoothness. In a jocular vein he said, 'Aray, yaar, aren't your hands just like a girl's?'

Minoo reacted as if he had been grossly insulted. With the speed of lightning, he brought out his knife. 'I warn you, if once more I hear you call me a girl, I'll kill you!'

Rajoo continued to stare, fascinated and puzzled at this beardless boy with soft and smooth fingers, with a lethal blade in his hand!

4

That night, while Moti kept guard over the open door, Rajoo slept on the floor, partly wrapped up in his torn jacket. Sometimes his legs would be uncovered, sometimes the head and shoulders. Feeling the cold, he sleepily folded his legs, looking like a human question mark.

But for Minoo there was no sleep. His wide open eyes were awake, though they couldn't see much in the dim half-light.

Rajoo muttered something incoherent in his sleep, unfolded his legs; there was a clatter as his foot hit an empty tin, and it rolled over. Minoo immediately sat up, tense and alert; his hand reached out for the knife beside him. But there was no one, only Rajoo sleeping in a funny position, contorting his body to keep warm. Minoo got up and draped his own blanket over Rajoo. The sleeping body felt the warmth, and he cosily nestled under the blanket.

From the distance came the dull thunder of the train. 'The 4 a.m. local,' thought Minoo. Taking a cotton bedsheet instead of his blanket, at last he too slept.

Moti got up, vigorously shook his head from side to side. Then he saw Rajoo who had kicked off the blanket. Taking an end between his teeth, the dog put it back over him. Then he turned to Minoo's bed and saw that it was empty. From outside came the sound of splashing water. Moti walked out of the door towards Minoo.

When Rajoo awakened, he was surprised to see the blanket, but his body was stiff because of the cold 'bed of stones' on which he had slept. He yawned, waved his arms and legs, and seeing Minoo's bed empty, marvelled at boys who got up so early. Then he heard the sound of splashing water.

'Well done, my boy,' he said as he came out in the backyard where, behind a banana tree, Minoo was bathing. 'You are duly bathed and ready for your morning prayers, I suppose. But my Guru's injunction was different! Never pray on an empty stomach. So, what about some breakfast?'

Minoo came out from behind the banana plant, water dripping from his short hair, a wet towel over his shoulders, and retorted, 'You are worried about breakfast, but to buy a meal, one needs some cash. Have you thought of that?'

'Don't you worry about it, Master Minoo,' Rajoo answered, splashing water over his face. 'Tonight when we set up our Great Indian Footpath Circus near the Bombay Carnival, there will be a shower of coins. You just wait and watch.'

5

The grounds of the carnival were ablaze with multicoloured lights. There were merry-go-rounds, giant wheels and magicians' booths, and plenty of other entertainment. Just near them was the humble Great Indian Footpath Circus of Rajoo, Minoo and Moti, but there was a sizeable crowd to watch their show, too.

When the show was over, Rajoo appealed to people to show their generosity. 'We don't charge tickets, our show is free, but we too must live and pay our grocer's bills,' he rattled on, shouting without a loudspeaker. 'So, kind friends, dear friends, generous friends, put your hands in your pockets and take out a coin—let it be twenty-five paisay, ten paisay, or five paisay.'

People were just fumbling for coins when two saucy girls, in hip-accentuating Maharashtrian saris, started singing to attract the crowd to their tamasha show. With their lilting, spicy song and tantalizing gestures, they were able to wean away the spectators from the Footpath Circus to their own show, for which already long queues were forming. Those who had put their hands in their pockets to take out a coin to put in Rajoo's hat now saved it to purchase a ticket for the tamasha. If the free preview provided by the two shameless hussies was any indication, thought Rajoo, here was entertainment that was bound to be popular.

Only a few child beggars remained to watch Rajoo and Minoo pack up their show. When he discovered only two small coins in his hat, Rajoo dropped them in the extended hands of the beggars!

When they returned home, all of them—Rajoo, Minoo and Moti—were hungry.

'What shall we eat tonight?' Minoo asked bitterly, once they had settled down.

'We shall eat nothing,' said Rajoo.

'Nothing?' repeated Minoo, surprised.

'Yes, Minoo, "nothing" is tastier than biryani, more spicy than the chaat that you get at Chowpatty, sweeter than jalebis and laddoos ...'

'Are you joking?' asked Minoo who was in no mood for humour.

'No, Minoo, I'm not joking at all. Like dal, bhaat, puri, kachori, pulao, qorma, "nothing", too, is a famous delicacy of our country which millions relish every day with great contentment.'

'All right, then,' shouted Minoo, still unable to appreciate Rajoo's sarcasm, 'our circus has failed. Now munch "nothing" for breakfast, eat "nothing" for lunch, and enjoy "nothing" for dinner.' Then, after a pause, 'Cursed be those tamasha players. They spoilt our show. God knows what special attraction they have inside their tent!'

'The attraction was not inside, but outside the tent, Master Minoo,' Rajoo explained to him. 'Didn't you see those saucy dames inviting people with songs and tantalizing gestures?'

Rajoo appraised Minoo. 'Master Minoo, we have everything in our circus.' Pointing to Moti, then to Minoo, and finally to himself, he said, 'We have the lion, we have the acrobat, and we have the clown. We are short of only one thing.'

'What's that?' Minoo asked.

Advancing towards Minoo, he replied, 'We need only a girl!'

'A girl?' Minoo spat out the word with great contempt.

'Yes, Minoo, if we also had a girl in our group, we could have knocked the stuffing out of those tamasha players.'

Now, face to face with Minoo, Rajoo touched the boy's cheeks. Minoo took a step back, but Rajoo continued to shout as if he had suddenly found a hidden treasure trove. 'What a fool I am not to think of it before! I tell you, you're a readymade girl, Minoo. Let me do your make-up and drape you in a nine-yard sari like those girls, and all the people will be mad after you!'

Hearing this, Minoo flushed with anger. 'Rajoo! I warn you—if you continue to talk like that, I'll—I'll—I'll kill you!'

'All right!' Taken aback by this hysterical threat, Rajoo tried to calm him down. 'If you say, I won't mention it again. What was there to be so angry about? I was only jokingly suggesting a possibility. Many of these tamasha girls used to be boys, some still are. But if you refuse to play-act as a female, we will recruit a real girl for our troupe.'

But Minoo did not welcome even this proposal. Indeed, he reacted almost as angrily as he had to the other suggestion. Bitterly he hissed, 'The day a girl enters our troupe, it will be the end of our friendship!'

Rajoo kept wondering why this boy had reacted so violently at the mere mention of a girl. Had he, too, suffered a bitter disappointment at so young an age?

6

Despite the previous evening's setback, they were again performing at the carnival. They had polished up their show and introduced new and more daring items which ensured a better clientele, despite the competition from the tamasha and other entertainment in their neighbourhood. Minoo was holding up a flaming ring through which Moti had to make a spectacular leap. Rajoo was shouting above the din of the carnival.

'See the amazing lion of Africa leap through the ring of fire. Now Master Minoo, the daring acrobat, will show you his most thrilling act. He will somersault and jump through a ring fitted with four deadly knives. These knives are sharper than the sharpest sword. Master Minoo is risking his young life just to thrill you and entertain you. Ladies, gentlemen and children, just watch Master Minoo.'

Rajoo held the ring fitted with four shiny knives through which Minoo, wearing a loose khaki shirt and shorts, had to jump. And he passed through the knives unscathed, but there was a quick sound of fabric being torn by one of the pointed knives. Minoo, getting up from the ground, nervously felt his shirt and found a big tear at a crucial place, and through it became visible those tell-tale curves which had been concealed so long. Minoo the boy was—a girl!

Rajoo saw this in a flash and understood the situation. So Minoo, the friend with whom he had become so informal and intimate, had turned out to be a girl! He felt, somehow, cheated and betrayed. After his two heartbreaks—caused by Mary and Marina—he had decided to keep his distance from women. And here he had been fooled by a slip of a girl masquerading as a boy, and had been living with her under the same roof for days and weeks.

Angrily he started moving towards Minoo who was lying helplessly on the ground, using her hand to cover the exposed bosom. But Minoo got up in a flash and ran from there. The merry-go-round, which was slowing down, was on her way, and she jumped on it. There were wooden horses, which moved up and down with the motion of the merry-go-round, and she climbed on as the circular platform moved on, along with the dummy horses. Rajoo, who was pursuing her, also jumped into the moving platform and ran round it as the merry-go-round gathered speed. At last he caught up with her. But between them was a riderless wooden horse. When it went up, it covered Minoo's torn shirt and the curves of her breasts, when it went down, they became disturbingly visible.

Above the din of the carnival, the loud music of the merry-go-round, and the screams and nervous laughter of the children, Minoo shouted as she pleaded with Rajoo: 'Listen to me, Rajoo. Believe me, I did not want to deceive you.'

But Rajoo's eyes were aflame with anger. He did not say anything; he kept staring at the wooden horse which was going up, going down, mocking him by revealing the obvious truth, which had so far remained unrevealed only to a simpleton like him.

Minoo kept pleading, 'Rajoo, please let me explain how I was forced to adopt this disguise.' But Rajoo had jumped from the speeding merry-go-round, and was swallowed up by the carnival crowds.

Now Minoo was left alone, alone in a crowd, struck dumb amidst all the noise, the music, and the shouting voices of the carnival.

The merry-go-round was revolving.

The carnival was revolving.

The whole world was revolving.

And, at the immobile centre of this revolving universe, there was the wild-eyed Minoo, wearing a torn shirt, and looking helpless and forlorn.

7

The whole night, in her hut, Minoo kept the door open, waiting for Rajoo. But Rajoo did not come home.

She stood by the open door, she sat by the window, keeping a lonely vigil. She lay on her cot, but couldn't sleep.

The dark night dissolved into the dim light of dawn. The trains began to pass along the distant railway lines. Still he did not come.

It was daylight when the familiar footsteps were heard. On seeing him, she got up. She noticed that he was carrying a packet in his hand.

She felt she had the right to complain: 'You've come now! Where were you the whole night?'

'In hell or heaven.' The fire of his anger had not cooled down. 'Who are you to ask me?'

'I am your friend—Master Minoo!'

'You are not Master Minoo, you are Miss Minoo and, therefore, you never were, and never will be, my friend.'

'For God's sake, what sin have I committed that you speak to me in that tone?'

'Minoo!' The frustration of years was in the voice of Rajoo as he spoke. 'That sin is called untruth. I have suffered much and endured much—I have reconciled myself to a life without love, without hope, but I cannot endure lies, I cannot reconcile myself to be fooled by untruth. Your "Master Minoo" was a lie, a fraud, and a deception.'

'All right!' Now Minoo also was losing her temper. 'It was a lie and a fraud. But do you know who was responsible for it? You. You! You!'

Rajoo was taken aback by the accusation. 'Me?'

'Yes—you!' Minoo's voice was charged with bitterness. 'If not you personally, then your whole fraternity of men. Men like you! Do you know what a helpless orphan girl has to go through in this man's world of yours? With what hopes and ambition I came to Bombay to work in films, become a great artiste, even a filmstar. But for a lonely girl, it is very difficult to preserve her self-respect and honour in the city. Wherever I went, I met wolves in human shape. Whoever looked at me felt I was easy game to prey upon. So I decided that, to protect my honour, I would have to die.' There was infinite sadness in her voice. 'The long-haired Meena was dead, and her place was taken by a knife-wielding boy of the streets. That's how I became Master Minoo!'

Now Rajoo spoke in a softer tone. 'But now there's no need to keep up the deception. Take this.' He offered her the packet which he'd brought.

'What is it?' Minoo—or Meena—asked as she took the packet.

'It is the shroud of the friendship of Rajoo and Minoo. Take off these rags which are nothing but lies. Wear this sari and confront the world truthfully.'

Taking out a mustard-coloured sari with a bright red border, Meena was lost in admiration. She seemed to be hearing some sweet, distant melody which brought a sad little smile to her lips.

She went behind a partition. Unfolding the sari, she felt it on her cheeks and then held it against her bosom. 'You've no idea after how many months the soft fabric of a sari has touched my body—you've no idea how I feel at this moment. It is like a rebirth.' Then she pulled down a chik-curtain and, behind it, took off her shirt and began to drape the sari around her body, talking nostalgically, animatedly, all the time. 'You won't believe it but this crude, foul-mouthed Master Minoo used to be a shy girl at one time. They said I was beautiful, too. At school I used to sing and dance, and everyone predicted that one day I would be a great actress whose beauty would dazzle onlookers.'

Then she came out, and Rajoo looked at her, fascinated. The curves and contours of her body were accentuated by the sari, which was draped without a blouse.

'Now do you see me in my true form?' she asked.

'Yes, but I didn't imagine I'd be so dazzled.' In his imagination, he was seeing Mary and Marina. And now Meena? No, no. He did not want a heartbreak for the third time. He won't be able to endure it. He must avoid it at all costs. He must go away, far away from her disturbing presence.

When he turned around to go out, Meena called out to him.

'Are you leaving?'

'Yes, Meena, I cannot stay.'

'You are leaving me?' In her voice there was an affectionate concern, as well as fear of being left alone.

'You were living alone before I came here. You can live alone after I am gone.'

'You don't realize that it was Master Minoo who could live alone because he could protect himself. Meena can't stay alone and unprotected.' Meena stood in his way, asserting her right. 'You've transformed Master Minoo into Miss Meena. You can't leave me. I won't let you go anywhere.'

'No, Meena, *please*.' Rajoo's twice-injured heart cried out. 'I've always lost the game of love, I have suffered a lot. This is a dangerous game, Meena.'

And now he could see the personification of those dangers, those beautiful, bewitching, haunting dangers. Mary and Marina and now, standing beside them, Meena.

He turned abruptly and stepped out. Was he running away from Meena, or from Mary and Marina? Or was he trying to run away from himself?

Meena's impassioned voice pursued him. 'Rajoo! Rajoo! Don't misunderstand my love, Rajoo!'

But Rajoo did not turn back.

The whole day Meena waited for Rajoo's return. The evening found her still waiting. Distraught and nervous, she scoured the whole locality, looking for Rajoo, but found no trace of him. Now she could no longer hide her emotions. Her love for Rajoo, the dependence upon his companionship, the fear of being alone—all these emotions found expression in a song that seemed to be the cry of her soul. At that moment she was passing through two storms. One was the storm within her heart and soul that had shaken her whole existence since Rajoo's discovery of her true identity. The other was a storm of the elements, wind and rain and thunder and lightning that proclaimed the advent of the monsoon. All night she battled with these storms, and even the squally downpour could not prevent her from searching for her Rajoo, because now she knew that without him her existence was incomplete.

Soaked to the skin, she continued to look for him till the rain abated towards the end of the night, and in the dim light of dawn she saw him silhouetted within the rim of one of the large drainpipes lying about, waiting to be buried in the ground.

Excited and happy, she ran up to him and fell down beside him. All her former reserve, all her strength of will, melted in his arms. By surrendering herself, she made him captive—she hoped, forever!

8

Now a new phase of life began for Rajoo.

So long as Rajoo and Minoo lived together as friends,

both of them shared the responsibility of running the household. But now, since the self-sufficient boy had been transformed into a delicate and beautiful girl, it became Rajoo's duty to stock the kitchen, Minoo only doing the cooking. Rajoo did not mind shopping, as he was used to doing this for his mother.

One morning when, loaded with the week's rations, vegetables, lentils, salt, sugar and a tin of cooking oil, Rajoo was entering the hut, a gentle command warned him from inside. 'Just wait outside. Don't come here. I am putting on my clothes.'

Rajoo was taken aback by this display of modesty and said somewhat peevishly, 'Then, hurry up. We have to plan a new show—there's a proposal for a qawwali programme that I want to discuss with you. While you dress, I will wait outside.'

Between the two parts of the room, the solitary sari bought by Rajoo had been hung to dry. Using that as a screen, Meena popped up her head and said, 'What happened? Why so sulky and cross?'

Rajoo heaved a sigh and replied, 'What has happened, Meena, is that this sari has become a wall between us.'

Meena looked at Rajoo coquettishly, then at the sari, and muttered to herself, 'Crazy fellow, calling a sari a wall!'

He came out and sat down near Moti. The dog, also feeling neglected, was lying on the ground.

Feeding him some biscuits which he had specially brought for him, Rajoo talked to Moti in a confidential tone. 'Come, Moti, I want to discuss something with you. They say dogs are more loyal than men, and often more intelligent. The point is, the situation is once again serious—almost critical. I have been sorely disappointed twice, don't want to be hurt a third time. What do you think I should do?'

Moti assumed a thoughtful posture but, before he could bark his reply, Meena come out of the partition. Rajoo got up, gaping wide-eyed and open-mouthed, dazzled by Meena's beauty. The same sari which, a moment ago, had served as a wall, was now draped around her in a most provocative fashion.

Meena, fully aware of the impression she was making, spoke in a voice husky with emotion. 'Now there is no wall between us, is there?'

Rajoo, still gaping at her, said, 'No, now there is no wall between us, Minoo.'

'Not Minoo, but Meena.'

'Meena.'

In Rajoo's eyes, and also in Meena's, there was desire, yearning, hunger and passion.

Rajoo took a step forward. His hands went

forward, towards Meena's cheeks, her face and body. He would have touched her, kissed her, taken her in his arms, but she moved a step backward.

Rajoo, disappointed, looked at her with enquiring eyes. 'Why?'

Meena looked at her newly washed body draped in a spotless sari, then pointed to Rajoo's hands which were stained with oil and grease and coal-dust.

Rajoo looked at his dirty hands, then at Meena's immaculate beauty, then at her face which seemed to be aglow with an inner flame, then took a step back and, switching off his emotion as only a joker could, said in a matter-of-fact tone, 'Let's talk about the offer we have for a qawwali programme!'

9

Instead of the 'Great Indian Footpath Circus', it was now the 'Grand Qawwali Programme Starring Queen of Qawwali Meena Bano Bhonchali and King of Qawwali Rajoo Qawwal'.

From the first day their programmes were a great success and the contractor who had arranged them paid them fifty rupees every night. Meena combined her flair for dancing with her qawwali, and people flocked to see her, for she brought new colour and verve to the usual singing of classical verses. But the life and soul of their show were the meaningful duets, the give and take, the sawal and jawab, of Rajoo and Meena, as they exchanged seemingly impromptu (but really well-rehearsed) poetic repartees, and made musical points and counterpoints.

They were comparatively well-off now. They had even acquired some items of second-hand furniture but kept living in the same hut that had proved lucky for them. It was the place where they had first met, shared their days of poverty and privations, and discovered their love for each other.

One day, counting the money before putting it in the cupboard, Rajoo said, 'Do you know, Meena, our qawwali has created a sensation in the city. Everyone is talking about Meena Bano Bhonchali and Rajoo Qawwal.'

Meena contradicted him. 'No. First Rajoo Qawwal, then his Meena. First the teacher and then the taught.'

'No, Meena,' said Rajoo, locking the cupboard, 'qawwali is like love. No one is first, and no one is second. Two voices, two tones, two melodies, that merge into one.' Suddenly he produced the little joker which he had secretly taken out of the cupboard. 'You don't believe me, ask him!'

'What is it?'

'Haven't you recognized it? This is me.'

'But this is a joker,' Meena said, doubtfully.

'So what? Joker—that's me! If you turn him upside down, he laughs. If you throw him in a corner, he laughs. If you ignore him, slap him, or beat him up, even then he laughs.'

Meena held the little joker close to her heart and asked, 'And if one lovingly embraces him, then?'

'Then, too, he laughs.'

'Then I will keep him forever with me.'

'Is your heart big enough to accommodate him?' asked Rajoo.

'Yes, Rajoo. How can you even doubt it?'

He couldn't believe it, because no other girl had been able to find a place for him—or for the little joker—in her heart. Possibly, Meena was different from the others. Could he, then, play the dangerous game of love with equanimity?

Still clasping the little joker to her bosom, Meena came very close to Rajoo. He could feel her hot breath on his face. Time stood still for a moment.

Then came the plaintive, wail-like yelping of Moti, the dog, as if he was crying out for help. The moment passed. The inexorable march of time was resumed.

Rajoo reacted to the dog's outcry. 'What's

happened to Moti?' he cried out, and ran to look for his mongrel.

The municipal van, full of stray dogs, was already moving away when Rajoo came out. He ran after the van to save his Moti, shouting, 'He is not a street dog, damn you!' But the truck gathered speed and disappeared in a cloud of dust.

Meena was playing with the doll when Rajoo entered. Seeing his downcast countenance, Meena enquired, 'What happened, Rajoo?'

'The municipal dogcatchers have taken away our Moti,' Rajoo replied, feeling bereaved. 'Now they'll kill him!'

Rajoo saw no signs of anxiety on the face of Meena. In a cold and unemotional voice she said, 'Yes, what else are they to do with street dogs?'

'Our Moti was not a street dog,' Rajoo reminded her of the pact that had been sealed between the three of them. 'He was a partner in our Footpath Circus.'

'But the Footpath Circus is no more,' Meena proclaimed. 'Now our *qawwali* is a hit. Why do we need Moti?'

Rajoo felt as if she had slapped him. A light flashed in his mind revealing, it seemed, the true face of Meena. He cried out, 'So you love someone only when you need him. When you needed Moti, you showered your love on him. Now that you don't, you have abandoned him, leaving him to be killed! Today it's Moti, tomorrow it will be me!'

Now Meena felt the grave implications of her foolish and callous remark. Looking at Rajoo, his face red with anger, she felt scared. 'Rajoo, Rajoo!' she pleaded and cried, 'forgive me, please. I never meant it in that sense. Please don't be cross with your Meena.' Then she held up the little joker. 'Look here, even he is requesting you to forgive me. This joker—who laughs even when he is angry!'

'Yes, the joker laughs, whatever happens!' he said and forced himself to smile.

But there was no happiness in his heart—only a strange disquiet, an unknown fear, black shadows of the days to come. But still, he was a joker. It was his business, his duty, his karma and his dharma to laugh and make people laugh. So he said aloud, 'See, I am laughing,' and Meena was satisfied that all was well. She did not know that this laughter was soaked in tears.

10

After finishing the qawwali, when Rajoo and Meena entered their dressing room, they found a flamboyant-looking character, waiting. He addressed them in the extravagant and flowery language of the Mughal courts, and introduced himself as 'Kalanarain Dilgeer, proprietor, Grand Theatrical Company'.

'What can we do for you?' Rajoo asked him when he got a chance to speak.

'If you join our theatre, we shall feel ourselves lucky. In no time, you two will eclipse all the other heroes and heroines.'

As soon as she heard the word 'heroines', Meena was all attention. 'You mean I can become a heroine?'

'Of course, Meena Bai,' the theatre owner assured her. 'I knew it the moment I saw you singing and dancing in the qawwali programme. You are a born artiste.'

Overjoyed, Meena turned to Rajoo. 'Did you hear that? Seth Saheb says I'm a born artiste.'

Before Rajoo could say anything, Munshi Dilgeer declared, 'I'll present the two of you in social plays, historical plays, operas, ballets, with absolutely new stage effects and haunting music.'

'Really?' was all that Meena managed to say.

'Then shall we say five hundred rupees a month for each of you?'

Rajoo felt it was too much and he exclaimed

in surprise, 'Five hundred rupees?' But the theatre owner misunderstood it to mean that he regarded five hundred rupees a month as contemptuously inadequate. He raised the price he was offering.

'All right. I'll make it six hundred rupees a month and we will prepare the contract right now. But there is only one condition—from today you'll not appear in a cheap entertainment like qawwali!'

Now Rajoo at last got a chance to speak. 'How can we get out of our qawwali commitments? How do you expect someone who has given us an advance, who has done advance bookings in our name, to agree to such a proposal, all of a sudden? We must think of him, too. It was he who brought us into qawwali.'

'We don't need to appear in qawwali programmes any more, Rajoo.' Meena had made up her mind. 'No, we'll work on the stage.'

What do we need Moti for?

Why do we need qawwali?

Why do I need Rajoo?

Rajoo already heard these words in his imagination.

But Meena, delirious with the fever of success, heard only one word: 'heroine'. And when she boarded the train—was it the train of her destiny?—with the theatre group, she heard it in the clatter of the speeding wheels, 'Heroine! Heroine! Heroine!'

The Grand Theatrical Company staged plays according to the taste of the local public.

In Lucknow they staged an opera on the life of Wajid Ali Shah.

Rajoo made a convincingly aristocratic Wajid Ali Shah, the colourful king of Oudh, who was not only a connoisseur of classical music but himself played superlatively on the pakhawaj. Meena became a homely and beautifully costumed court dancer who had to observe the decorum of the court while performing in the royal presence.

During the opera, Meena, as the court dancer, sat at the feet of the king, and Rajoo, in royal accents, said to her, 'Not there, Laila. Come and sit near us.'

'Your Majesty,' Laila—that is Meena—replied respectfully, 'my place is at your feet.'

'No, Laila, you are enthroned in our heart,' Wajid Ali Shah said to Laila—or was it Rajoo to Meena?

Meena forgot it was all play-acting, and softly whispered, 'Really, Rajoo?'

'Yes, Meena.' Rajoo, too, chose to give a new twist to the dialogue in the play. 'For ever and ever, you shall be the queen of my heart.'

The spectators gave a resounding ovation at the end of the performance.

Time, the great revolutionary, dethrones kings and

snatches their crowns—on the stage, as in real life. Rajoo discovered it all too soon.

When they came to the Lucknow railway station to take the train to the next destination, Meena found herself accommodated in a single-berthed air-conditioned coupé. When she enquired, 'But what about Rajoo?' she was told, 'We could get only two adjacent coupés in the air-conditioned coach—so we reserved one for you and one for Seth Saheb.'

This Seth Saheb was not only the financier of the theatre, but the virtual owner. Meena had seen him as an odiously fat and oily creature who had diamond rings on his fingers, and always reeked of alcohol.

Feigning surprise, Meena asked, 'Oh, is Seth Saheb also coming along with us? I thought he was too preoccupied with his many businesses.'

'That he is, indeed,' the manager said obsequiously, 'but when Seth Saheb gets interested in a heroine—I mean in her career—he sacrifices his commercial interests for the sake of the theatre.'

Meena had heard much about men of money who owned, or financed, theatrical or cinema companies and their special interest in the 'career' of their heroines. When she became thoughtful, the manager left her with the ominous information, 'Seth Saheb is in the next compartment. If you need anything, you have just to knock on his door.'

Meena was saying, 'Look here ... I mean ...' but the manager had already disappeared down the corridor.

Now she looked around the small compartment and at the door which opened into the other coupé. The latch was down; anyone could come from the other side. Thinking this, she got up to pull the latch when the door started opening. Nervously, she retreated but in the narrow coupé there was space enough for only one step. Through the open door entered Seth Saheb, obviously inebriated, with his moustaches that owed their blackness to a hair-dye, and the ebony-dark face which was his natural complexion. He held his hands in front of him, and the diamonds on his fingers sparkled in the light.

Seth Saheb was unabashedly ogling at Meena, appraising her.

Meena was taken aback by this sudden and unwelcome intrusion. She didn't know what to do, what to say.

Seth Saheb's lips, under the thick moustaches, quivered, revealing irregular teeth stained with paan and tobacco.

At last Meena said, 'Please be seated.'

Seth Saheb made himself comfortable on the berth, near the window. Casually, he pulled down the blinds. Then, he asked Meena, too, to sit down.

Meena could see, beyond the glass panel of the door, Rajoo standing in the corridor, and beckoning to her.

She made gestures of helplessness. How could she get away when the seth was there?

Seth Saheb, watching this silent exchange, got up. Meena heaved a sigh of relief. She thought the man of money was going back to his coupé. But he had no such intention. He just pulled the curtain to cover the glass panel. A bit of cloth again became a wall separating Rajoo and Meena!

Resuming his seat, the seth eyed the curtain to make sure there was no hole for peeping toms. 'Shameless fellows! Peeping and parading whenever they see a pretty face!' Then, looking at Meena sitting at the edge of the seat, preparing to rise any moment, he said, 'Be comfortable.'

Meena slid back on the seat a few inches to reassure him she was not going to run away—just yet!

'You are a wonderful dancer, Miss Meena.' Then Seth Saheb took a paan out of the silver box he kept in the pocket of his silk kurta.

'That's very kind of you, Seth Saheb, otherwise I am only a beginner.'

'No, no', the seth insisted, 'all the paperwallas say the same thing—that Miss Meena is incomparable. I have given your photos for publication. After all, when we get such a good artiste, we must do much publicity for her to make her name and fame known to the public.'

'Thank you, Seth Saheb.'

'What is all this "thank you" business, Meena?' It seemed safe enough to drop the 'Miss'. Further emboldened, he placed his ebony-black hand, sparkling with diamonds, on top of her fair and delicate fingers as if he were just patting her. 'After all, this theatre belongs to you—I mean to artistes like you!'

Meena gently slid her hand from under his perspiring palm.

The seth decided to try another conversational approach. 'That jewellery you wore for that dance—how do you like it?'

Meena knew they were crude, the jewels fake, but she said, 'They are very beautiful.'

'Then you keep them with you. So long as you are in our company, we want you to wear them.'

Now Meena had to thank Seth Saheb.

'Again this "thank you" business?' Seth Saheb shouted a complaint. 'After all, to whom does this whole company belong?'

Meena assumed an appropriately coquettish pose and said what he wanted to hear. 'It's mine.'

'Well done. Now you are fully qualified to be a heroine.' Then he got up, satisfied that Meena was slowly coming round to an amenable attitude. But he never wanted to hustle a girl. For he knew the inevitable would happen. So, giving her a farewell smile, he went into his coupé, and closed the door. He did not latch his side, but Meena slowly moved forward and noiselessly slid the latch.

Then she opened the door, and went out into the corridor, at the other end of which she could see the silhouette of Rajoo, standing against the window.

11

Meena went up to him and whispered, 'Rajoo! Rajoo!' But Rajoo did not answer, nor did he look at her. He continued to look out of the window though there was nothing to see except the blackness of the night through which the train was passing.

'Rajoo,' she called out again, 'why don't you speak?'

Now Rajoo looked back at her. His face was in the shadows, so Meena could not see the despair that was in the depth of his eyes. Then he turned again to the windowpane.

'Rajoo! What are you looking at?'

At last he spoke. 'I'm watching the world receding fast.'

'You're able to see in the dark?'

'One's eyes get dazzled by the footlights on the stage. Then one begins to see clearly in the dark.'

Meena knew what Rajoo was implying, but she assumed an innocent pose. 'I don't know what you mean.'

'Knowledge is dangerous—sometimes it can be fatal!'

Meena impulsively kissed his hand. 'What I do know is that I love you, Rajoo—only you!'

'And who says that?'

'This is your Meena, Rajoo!'

'And was it another Meena who has just come from a cosy chat with Seth Saheb, behind drawn curtains?' At last he spat out the poison in him.

'So it's that!' Meena said coquettishly. 'Men are so suspicious and so jealous! How could I know Seth Saheb would drop in for a chat. He is the virtual owner of the theatre. I couldn't, after all, refuse to talk to him.'

'How could you?' Rajoo spoke now with all the bitterness of his heart. 'And that, too, when the air-conditioned coupés are side by side, with a communicating door, and a curtain to discreetly pull across the door when you need privacy. What more can a couple of lovers want?'

Meena knew that whatever Rajoo was saying was bitter but basically not unjustified. She was conscious of her own weakness, born of opportunism. She couldn't afford to tell off the seth, because she desperately wanted a career in the theatre—eventually in films. It was the fever of success. So, to smother her sense of guilt, she desperately clung to Rajoo, covering him with kisses, and frantically whispered, 'Rajoo! Rajoo! I don't want anything in the world except your love—neither name nor fame nor fortune. If you don't want me to work in this theatre, I'll leave it this minute. Together, we'll restart our Footpath Circus.'

'Meena!' Rajoo said gently but firmly, removing her arms from his neck. 'Moti is dead. So is our Footpath Circus. Now you are a famous heroine, used to air-conditioned luxury.'

'Do you want to test my loyalty?' Meena asked

in desperation. 'Then, here you are!' She sprang to pull the alarm chain. But Rajoo caught her hand in time; there was a tussle in the narrow, deserted corridor; Meena angrily scratched him with her long tapering nails, and it was then that Rajoo gave her a resounding slap on her cheek. She started crying helplessly, leaning on his shoulder.

Patting her gently on the back, Rajoo said, 'Don't play-act all the time, my dear. It's not good for your health or for your good looks!'

12

The operatic *Heer Ranjha* which they presented in the different cities of the Punjab was a play, but it also presented a play within a play.

Heer—that is Meena—sat in her bridal chamber dressed in silks and brocades, with flowers strewn on her nuptial bed. Ranjha—that is Rajoo—dressed in the saffron robes of renunciation, came there, singing a mendicant's song of devotion, begging from door to door.

Heer, recognizing his voice, called out guiltily: 'Ranjhe!'

Ranjha now came inside, and answered in Waris Shah's immortal verses.

Yar bad nitiya,
Changi koi na kitiya
Sadha dil mode dey.

(Oh, my faithless friend,
Give me back my heart.)

Heer (or Meena) cried as she answered:

Dosh koi na teri Heer da
Rab mel kita, Rab dur kita
Aite khel sara taqdeer da.

(Blame not your luckless Heer,
It was God who united us, God that separated us,
It's all a game of our destiny.)

Now Heer and Ranjha, Meena and Rajoo, confronted each other.

After a little silent pause, not Ranjha but Rajoo spoke to not Heer but Meena: 'Why do you blame God? Don't hold destiny responsible for your doings!'

Meena cried out, 'Don't misunderstand me,' and softly whispered, 'Rajoo!'

And Rajoo replied, 'Didn't I tell you, knowledge and understanding can be fatal, Meena?'

The warm-hearted Punjabi audience, who knew nothing about the play-within-the-play, cheered and applauded, praised the natural and emotional singing and acting of Rajoo and Meena, which had brought to life the legendary characters of Ranjha and Heer!

The wheels of the train thundered across the country and brought their theatre to Madras, and Meena's fame and popularity soared higher and higher. In Lucknow, Rajoo was Wajid Ali Shah, the King of Oudh, and Meena was a court dancer in his durbar. In the Punjab, they were Heer and Ranjha, lovers and equals. In Madras, Meena danced as a glamorous princess, and Rajoo, made up as a south Indian musician, was humbly and inconspicuously seated among others in the orchestra.

While she danced, Meena's eyes were on the packed hall, and on the distinguished and discriminating audience representing the cream of Madras aristocracy and intelligentsia. Among them, in the front row, she was thrilled to recognize the famous actor–director–producer Kumar. This was too good to be true. What was he doing there?

Seeing the great filmstar, Meena felt she had reached the climax of her career as a dancer and a stage actress. Her dance acquired, besides the classical purity of the mudras, a verve and bodily abandon that, she calculated, would not fail to attract and fascinate a film producer.

Rajoo, appreciative but critical, was watching her movements. She was dancing very well, but with a little extra intensity, as if it were her last performance.

Meena's dance was now reaching the climax. The whole house was applauding, the curtain was falling and rising again. Meena was receiving encore after encore and acknowledging it with folded hands, but her eyes were fixed on only one person who, she noted with satisfaction, was applauding most enthusiastically.

When the curtain finally came down, she cried out, taking off her ghungroos, 'Rajoo! Can you guess whom I spotted in the auditorium?'

Rajoo had no time to reply from his place in the orchestra corner when a whole crowd came in through the stage entrance—the theatre proprietor, manager, dance master, photographers, autograph hunters. And in the midst of them all, the tall and handsome Kumar, the idol of millions.

Seeing him coming in, Meena was so excited that the ghungroos fell from her hand with a merry jingle and she completely forgot that, a moment earlier, she had been talking to Rajoo. She was dumbfounded with the ecstasy of the moment.

'Miss Meena,' the proprietor said, 'please garland the chief guest of the evening.'

A garland was handed over to Meena. With her heart beating fast, she went near Kumar. The photographers focused their cameras, but she had hardly raised her hand to garland Kumar when he made a gesture to restrict her. 'This evening, it is you who deserves all garlands.' Saying this he took the garland from her and placed it around her neck.

The photographers clicked their cameras, the flashguns flashed, and they were all herded outside along with the teenage fans and autograph-hunters.

'Thank you, thank you very much, Kumar Saheb,' Meena stuttered out of nervous excitement.

'You know my name?'

'Who doesn't know you?'

'They all know me,' he heaved a dramatic, deep sigh, 'but few recognize me!'

Meena said gushingly, 'I've been your devoted fan for a long time. But I didn't expect you in Madras. Your studio is in Bombay.'

'I've come here in connection with the casting of a new film. Had to interview several aspirants.' And then he caught her by the hand. 'Please come outside.'

Taking her to a corner of the stage, he casually

dismissed the theatre owner, 'Excuse me, please. I want to talk to Miss Meena, if you don't mind.'

'Of course, of course. Go ahead, Kumar Saheb.'

And then turning to his manager, 'Come on, let's not disturb the conversation of two great artistes.'

The two great artistes were now face to face. Kumar came straight to the point. 'Would you like to work with me in a film?'

Meena was stunned with the suddenness of it. She did not know what to say. The whole world seemed to be spinning crazily, and her head was spinning along with it. At last she managed to say, 'You mean I will get a chance to work with you?'

'Of course,' he replied, sure of himself, and also sure of her response. 'But first there must be a screen test. Can you take tomorrow's plane to Bombay?'

'Ji?' She could not tell if it was a dream or reality. 'Do I have to leave tomorrow?'

'Yes, tomorrow.' The star–producer spoke with the self-confidence of a jet-set go-getter. 'Because today's last plane to Bombay has already left! Your ticket will be delivered to you tomorrow morning.'

It was only now that Meena remembered Rajoo. She said, 'Kumar Saheb, not one ticket—but two—Rajoo will also go with me.' Then she looked around for the missing one. 'Rajoo! Rajoo!' When he emerged, from his shadowy corner, she complained, 'Rajoo, where were you! I've been searching for so long. I don't know where you get lost.'

'I was near you,' replied Rajoo, 'but you never looked back.'

Now Meena had to introduce Rajoo. 'Kumar Saheb, this is—er—my friend Rajoo. Whatever I know I've learnt from him.'

Kumar was going to make some remark when Rajoo said with folded hands, 'It's very kind of Meena-ji to say so, but it's not true. On the other hand, I learnt a great deal from her!'

But Meena was too full of her good fortune to notice the sting in his remark. She went on enthusiastically, 'Did you hear, Rajoo, Kumar Saheb is giving me a chance as a heroine in his next film. Isn't it wonderful? We're flying to Bombay tomorrow.'

'Tomorrow?' Rajoo exclaimed at the suddenness of the decision. 'But what will happen to the theatre?'

Meena replied without hesitating or fumbling for an answer, 'Who needs a career in theatre when one is getting a chance in films?'

Kumar paid no attention to their discussion—even if he did, he didn't show it. He pronounced his verdict. 'All right, Miss Meena. Two tickets will be delivered to you tomorrow morning. But remember one thing, please, so there's no misunderstanding afterwards, my heart is not part of the bargain with my artistes. I don't let my emotions interfere with my profession, goodbye.'

Then he went away, as self-confident as ever. Rajoo and Meena were left on the empty stage, with all its ornate decorations of the temple set. Rajoo noticed that behind her was the bronze image of Nataraj, the God of Dance, and in front of her were the carvings of flying horses. Pygmies were trying to hold the reins of the winged steeds.

Now Meena could ask, 'Rajoo, tell me, have I made a mistake?'

'No,' said Rajoo, 'you've made no mistake.'

'Then, tell me, what should I do?'

'You do what Kumar Saheb has told you. Don't let your emotions interfere with your profession.' Then he looked at those flying horses. 'No one can hold back the reins of your winged steed. Aim high, with no regrets and without inhibitions, till you reach the seventh heaven of success.'

Meena now knew the hurt she had caused Rajoo. But she could only say, 'Rajoo!' In that one word, and the way she uttered it, was fully conveyed her ability to live up to her love!

But Rajoo was looking at the flying horses which,

one day, would carry her to dizzy heights—and away from him.

13

That day was yet far, though they were already being carried by the combined power of several thousand flying horses.

Two aeroplane tickets had been delivered, but Meena's seat was far removed from Rajoo's.

Meena had a VIP seat in front, next to Kumar Saheb. Rajoo had a seat allotted to him far in the rear.

As the plane flew at six hundred miles per hour, it was steady and silent. Most of the passengers were dozing—but not this trio, who were among the few reading newspapers or magazines. Silently, they were thinking their respective thoughts as they idly turned over the pages.

Kumar was reading *Fortune* and was thinking that it was one's material possessions that determined a man's destiny.

Meena was scanning through *Time* and secretly congratulating herself that the auspicious time had come to make the most momentous decision of her life.

And Rajoo was browsing through *Life* and thinking about the ups and downs, the light and shade, in one's existence. Life, he thought, is like a long, dark tunnel—or is it a long corridor? —and no one knows what is at the other end of it.

The corridor in Kumar Studio was long and seemingly unending, like life itself. At one end was a bench on which sat Rajoo, waiting—how many hours had it been?—for Meena. At the other end, a hundred feet away but what seemed a hundred miles to Rajoo, was the make-up room where Meena was being 'made-up' (or remade-up, thought Rajoo) for her screen test.

The room—the personal make-up room of the actor–director–producer—was large, air-conditioned and tastefully furnished. As she sat in front of a large mirror with a make-up man and a lady hair-dresser in attendance, Meena promised herself that a day could come when she would have a room just like this one. Behind her chair sat Kumar himself, critically looking at Meena's face in the mirror as it went through the long and intricate processes of the beautician's art. Meena, who could see Kumar in the mirror, turned round to face him.

'What are you looking at me for?' Kumar pointed at the mirror. 'Look there.'

'There, too, I can see you,' Meena made an effort at flattery. 'On every side, I see your reflection.'

'Look here, Meena,' Kumar propounded his egotistical philosophy, 'don't look at others. Look at yourself. Take interest in yourself, your beauty, your face, your figure, your make-up, your costumes, your lines of dialogue, your scene, your picture. In short, learn to love yourself. There is nothing more important.'

Meena only partly understood what Kumar was saying. But, anyway, she looked hard at her own reflection and was pleased by the transformation the make-up man and the hairdresser had brought about. 'Now I really look beautiful,' she thought. 'When Rajoo sees me, how happy he'll be!'

Rajoo was still waiting on that same bench in the corridor when Meena stepped through an inner door which led to the large hall that served as a repository for costumes. On every side were glass cupboards full of dresses—saris, ghagras, cholis, blouses, pants, shirts, coats, suits, police uniforms and military uniforms, Rajput dresses, Arab dresses and fantastic dresses that belonged to no country and no culture, and had been used in dream sequences.

Kumar selected a chiffon sari and asked Meena to go into the dressing room and change. She dutifully obeyed, and when she came out, she thought she really looked chic and smart in the sari. 'When Rajoo sees it,' she thought, 'he'll surely like it, and the way I have worn it.'

Kumar was waiting for her but, when he saw her, he evidently did not like the simple and loose way the sari had been draped by Meena. He took a few safety pins, took off the palloo, tightened the drapery, fastened the folds with pins, and Meena saw in the mirror that the sari had been transformed into a body-clinging dress accentuating and revealing all her contours. She was not displeased with the result. It seemed to please Kumar, and that's what mattered at that time. 'Miss Meena,' said Kumar, explaining his point of view, 'the purpose of a sari or any dress is not to cover the beauty, but to reveal it!'

From the dress room, they walked into the moulder's workshop, where Meena saw a craftsman at work on the statue of a semi-nude woman, required for a set decoration. Kumar, out to impress his new heroine, asked the moulder to stand aside while he played about with the clay figure, squeezing one part, pinching another, depressing at one place, and raising at another. The body certainly became more daringly beautiful as the curves of the naked breasts became more pronounced. 'Isn't it better now, Meena?' He was seeking her approbation now.

Meena was subtle in her flattery. 'You're such a great artiste, and you can do all this!' She pointed to the remoulded clay statue. 'You have really given it a new personality. I wish you could do the same for me, Kumar Saheb.'

'Just wait till I start moulding you,' he said and looked at Meena as if she was not a girl of flesh and blood but a clay figure which he had just shaped and which only needed a few finishing touches before it would come to life.

They walked out into the studio compound where Kumar's long, sleek, limousine was waiting.

'Meena, you've worked hard today. Feel tired?'

'No, not particularly tired, Kumar Saheb.'

'Come, I'll take you for a drive to Juhu. We might have a cup of tea at Sun 'n' Sand. Have you any objection?'

'No.'

'Then, let's go.'

He took the wheel, she sat by his side, and the powerful car shot out of the studio gates, picking up speed in no time.

But Rajoo was still waiting in the corridor, waiting for Meena to emerge from the make-up room. It was growing dark now and the watchman, when he came to switch on the lights, asked him, 'Eh, Mister, what are you doing here?'

Rajoo felt self-conscious, and even humiliated, as he answered, 'I am waiting for Miss Meena. She is in that make-up room.'

The watchman told him that she had been gone for some time.

'No, no, it can't be. You must have seen someone else and mistaken her for Meena.'

'No, Mister, we don't make such mistakes. I have seen this Miss Meena of yours going in the car with Kumar Saheb—yes, I have seen it with my own eyes!'

It was like the curtain going up on a new act of the drama—earlier than he had expected!

Rajoo remembered the scene at the hotel the previous evening when they had just checked in. Kumar's secretary was with them and he had led them to a luxurious suite which had been reserved for Meena. As for Rajoo, the secretary had instructed the bellboy, 'Take Mr Rajoo's luggage to Room No. 812.'

'But,' Meena lodged a feeble protest, 'Rajoo always stays with me.'

'Kumar Saheb has reserved a separate room for

him on the same floor,' insisted the secretary. The bellboy carried away Rajoo's battered old suitcase and the khaki haversack.

Rajoo said, 'Let it be, Meena. Kumar Saheb has reserved for me an even more luxurious suite than yours.'

That night, seated in his room which was so small, it was like a cubicle, Rajoo received a phone call. 'Hello,' he spoke into the mouthpiece. 'Who?—Oh, Meena! What is it?'

The excited voice came over the wires. 'Oh Rajoo. What a grand suite Kumar Saheb has taken for me—it must be costing at least Rs 200 per day. How's your room, by the way?'

Rajoo looked round the little place and replied, 'Oh, it's very good.'

'Isn't Kumar Saheb very kind and considerate?' Meena wanted a confirmation of her opinion. 'How well he's looked after our comforts.'

And Rajoo laughed into the phone, though there was not even the flicker of a smile on his face. 'Especially my comforts! But tell me, how are you feeling?'

'Rajoo, I feel scared.'

'You feeling scared in a hotel room?' Rajoo expressed his surprise. 'Why, you didn't feel scared even in that haunted shack of yours!'

'There I wasn't alone, Rajoo. First I had Moti. Then I had you.' Rajoo smiled at his being bracketed with a faithful dog. 'I feel scared here, in these big rooms.'

Closing the mouthpiece with his hand, Rajoo murmured, 'This is just the first stage of success. The rooms will steadily grow bigger, the heart will steadily grow smaller—till it will hardly feel anything.'

Meena's voice pleaded with him, 'Rajoo, please. Unless you come and put me to sleep, I'll be awake the whole night!'

'Meena, you don't understand,' Rajoo explained to her. 'In these big, respectable hotels, it's forbidden for a man to go into a woman's room so late at night. This is the law of this hotel, of this world!'

Meena had said, 'But I must meet you—at least see you—I'm coming out in the corridor.'

In the deserted carpeted corridor, each hotel guest had kept his shoes outside the room to be polished in the morning. In front of some rooms there were pairs of shoes—one pair of man's shoes, one pair of lady's shoes or sandals.

Meena came running into Rajoo's arms and frantically clung to him. Then she pointed to the two pairs of shoes in front of a door. 'Rajoo, look there!'

Rajoo smiled at 'his' and 'her' shoes, and whispered, 'For that you need a licence—a marriage certificate!'

'Is that, too, a law?'

'Yes, Meena. That's the law. Now you be a good girl and go to your room and sleep.'

'But how will I sleep, unless someone puts me to sleep?'

'You will go to sleep, dreaming the dreams of your success. From now on, the song of success will be your lullaby.'

Meena, sulky and sullen, had gone back to her room. The whole corridor echoed the bang with which she closed the door. Rajoo heard that bang and addressed Meena in his thoughts:

'One day, my dear, you will close the door of your heart, too, with the same bang of finality.'

Now he knew that when someone closes the door of one's heart, you can hear no bang of finality. But you can feel it, because suddenly life becomes empty and desolate like that long, narrow, deserted corridor.

14

When Meena returned to her hotel suite at night and unlocked the door, in the dark she could see a familiar outline standing by the window. She switched on the lights.

'Rajoo! What are you doing here?'

'Waiting,' Rajoo replied without bitterness or rancour, even producing a sad little smile. 'Now that is the only thing I can do.'

'I am sorry, Rajoo, I was in a hurry when I left the studio ...'

'But you were not in a hurry when you returned at midnight?'

'What do you mean?'

'I mean that ... let it be! Who put this red rose in your hair?'

'What does it matter who put it? Is it a crime to put a rose in one's hair?'

'No, no, who says that? I say, it's great social service. That's why I want to know the name of that kind and thoughtful man—even if it's unnecessary!'

'What are you talking about?'

Rajoo was deriving a masochistic pleasure by turning the knife in his own wound. 'But I wonder why your precious Kumar Saheb didn't escort you to your room. Is his concern for his heroine discreetly restricted to a farewell in the hotel lobby?'

'He came all the way from Juhu to leave me here. Fifteen miles is quite a distance!'

'Fifteen miles?' He calculated the distance between them, as they stood at different ends of the room.

'Why, even fifteen feet can be a long distance which some people can't cover. But I am sure you must have eliminated many distances tonight.'

'What's the matter with you, Rajoo?' Meena was on the verge of tears. 'Do you think that in two days I've fallen in love with Kumar Saheb?'

Rajoo sighed. 'Love isn't bound by time, Meena. It can blossom in two minutes, or it does not take root even in two years!'

'Rajoo, what is it that you want? Shall I fall at your feet and apologize?'

'Meena, I want you—' He took a step towards her, then stopped. 'Meena, I want you to rehearse that scene which you have to perform before the cameras tomorrow. I don't want you to flunk your screen test. It's a passionate love scene and, to do it well, you better learn the meaning of love.'

For the first time, Meena saw in those kindly, loving eyes a glint of insane passion, which frightened her.

15

The lightweight curtains were flying in the night breeze coming through the open windows, and their shadows were making grotesque moving patterns on the walls.

Meena, in her revealing night dress, was lying in the middle of the carpeted bedroom, her fear-haunted eyes watching the demoniac figure of Rajoo advancing towards her prostrate figure.

'No, no,' Meena screamed, 'if you have no feeling for my chastity, at least think of your own honour and integrity. I had once seen in your face the vision of God.'

'Then behold today, in the same face, the vision of the Devil!' Rajoo looked wild, reckless, passionate, his eyes bloodshot. 'Tomorrow you are going to be the wife of a prince. But, before that, won't you accept the offering of love from your poor but loyal devotee?'

'No, no,' Meena pleaded tearfully, 'I had only come to bid you goodbye, to tell you I'm going tomorrow, Rajoo.'

Rajoo shouted in anger, 'Forgotten the dialogue again? Not Rajoo but Nirmal, Nirmal, Nirmal!' Now he revealed the bunch of papers in his hand. 'You will have to speak only what is written in the script, and nothing else.'

Meena got up to her feet and came up to Rajoo. Looking into his eyes, she said, 'What can I do, Rajoo? I am used to uttering only this name—Rajoo! Rajoo! Rajoo!'

'You'll have to forget this name, fling it out of

your heart, erase it from your memory!' Rajoo thundered, and then flung the papers at her. 'If you don't remember the dialogue, read the lines from the script.'

'No, not any more, Rajoo. I'm exhausted.'

Rajoo, himself exhausted, whispered grimly, 'Time is running out for both of us. We have only got tonight!' Then, in a more practical tone he said, 'Come on, rehearse your dialogue.'

Meena read from the dialogue sheet, mechanically, restlessly, 'No, no. I had only come to bid you goodbye, to tell you I'm going tomorrow.'

Rajoo parodied her listless manner. '*I'm going tomorrow*. While saying it, don't you feel anything?'

Meena sulked like a child. 'Then you tell me how I should speak these lines.'

'Every word must come out of your heart. First think about the situation, then understand its emotional significance, only then speak. What does a girl feel when she is going to abandon her lover? What should she feel? The writer has very appropriately described the mood. Read it.'

Meena read from the script. 'She will feel guilty and ashamed. Her eyes will be downcast. She will have difficulty in articulating her words.'

'Then feel all this and only then speak.'

Now Meena spoke with all the intensity of real—or simulated—emotion: 'Nirmal, I am going away tomorrow. But I am carrying your memory in my heart.'

Rajoo, too, spoke the cues with genuine feeling, 'Go, Rajni, go. Be happy wherever you are ...'

'Don't talk of happiness, Nirmal. True happiness I have found only in your company. From the beginning I've loved you alone, Rajoo.'

Again Rajoo lost his temper. 'Again forgetting the dialogue. It's unpardonable for an actress. Not Rajoo but Nirmal! Nirmal! Nirmal! If you want to be a filmstar, Meena, you'll have to follow the script.'

Meena flung the script. The sheets of paper flew away in the wind, like a flight of white pigeons. She shouted back. 'Not Nirmal, but Rajoo! Rajoo! Rajoo! I am saying all this to you. Can't you understand?'

She flung herself at Rajoo and, clinging to him, she said, 'I mean it, Rajoo. For the first and last time I have loved you and only you. Why don't you believe me? Why can't you trust me?'

With infinite tenderness, Rajoo caressed her hair, then he gently led her to the French windows draped with heavy curtains. He pulled aside those curtains. Outside, there was the streak of sunrise in the cloudy sky.

'Look there, Meena,' he said, pointing, 'the sun is about to rise.'

16

The darkness of the studio was engulfed by the artificial light of the arc lamps.

For the screen test, Meena had to speak the dialogue she had rehearsed with Rajoo. She spoke the lines as she faced the camera; she was surrounded by powerful arc lamps and other studio lights, but the impact of the previous night's emotional encounter had produced a peculiar expression of dramatic resignation on her face, and given a certain passionate tone to her voice that invested her performance with a piquant quality. The cameraman, the assistants, the sound recordists and the light coolies were all fascinated by this new artiste who could act with the emotional intensity of a veteran.

When the scene finished, everyone praised her acting, her intonation, the quality of her voice.

Meena waited for the verdict of Kumar, but he said nothing. So, in utter disappointment, she said, 'Kumar Saheb, shall I take off my make-up and go?'

'Yes, you must be tired after the day's work,' he said casually. 'Go and rest in the hotel. Tomorrow morning you have to face the press.'

'A press conference?' Meena could not contain her surprise and her pleasure. 'You mean that ...'

'It means that tomorrow I shall introduce my new heroine to the press. You've passed all the tests, now only one remains.'

She had been overjoyed, but then there was the additional suspense. 'What shall I have to do for that?' she asked nervously.

'For that you'll have to do nothing,' Kumar replied. 'For this test only your Rajoo is needed. Please send him to see me in the morning.' Then she was dismissed. He turned round to give instructions to his technicians and assistants. Meena did not have the nerve to ask him if Rajoo, too, was going to be screen-tested.

That evening when she saw Rajoo, she told him, 'Tomorrow Kumar Saheb has called you to the studio. He wants to talk to you.'

'About you?'

'About me or about you,' Meena replied. 'Or, maybe, about both of us.'

17

Meena was not there but her presence was overpoweringly felt.

Life-sized enlargements of her photographs in various costumes, different moods and different postures, taken as a part of the screen test, were set up on easel stands, arranged all round the empty floor of the studio. The still photographer, who had prepared the enlargements, was displaying them for Kumar's approval when Rajoo entered the studio.

'Come, come, Rajoo Saheb,' Kumar spoke with extra cordiality, 'I was just waiting for you. Please take this chair.' Then he dismissed the photographer. 'I'll call you later.'

He lowered himself in a chair beside Rajoo. Taking out his golden cigarette case, he offered it to him.

'No, thanks. I don't smoke.'

'You don't mind if I do,' said Kumar, taking out a cigarette and, taking for granted his guest's approval, he lighted it, and puffed out a cloud of smoke.

Across this smoke screen, he said, 'Now we can talk like two friends who are interested in the same ...'

Inevitably, both of them looked at the series of

portraits. Meena, too, it seemed, was made a party to their conversation.

Taking a cue from the photographs, Kumar said, 'Miss Meena speaks very highly of you. She says you've made a great name in the world of entertainment—pantomime, circus, qawwali, theatre, opera. But I am sorry, I have never seen any demonstrations of your histrionics.'

Now Rajoo looked at the many faces of Meena. 'Perhaps you've seen it but haven't recognized it as any creation.'

Whether he understood the implications of the remark or not, Kumar did not react. Calmly, he said, 'I want to ask you a question if you don't mind.'

'Go ahead,' said Rajoo, knowing what was coming next.

Kumar looked into his eyes and asked point-blank, 'Do you happen to love Meena?'

Rajoo looked steadily at Kumar as he said, 'Do I love Meena? A more appropriate question would be: do I love? And the answer is: yes. I love—everything and anything in this world. I love men and women and children, I love trees and flowers and stones …'

With a sarcastic smile, Kumar interrupted him, 'Among these flowers and stones, is there a girl named Meena?'

With a visible softening of expression and tone, Rajoo said, 'Yes, there is.'

'Then let me tell you something.' Kumar got up and began pacing restlessly. 'Meena can become a great film artiste …'

Rajoo interrupted him. 'You mean you can make her a great film artiste.'

'Yes,' Kumar asserted without hesitation, 'but if you remain with her, she'll never realize all her potential. She'll always be subdued, inhibited, by your presence.'

'And now can I put the same question to you?' Rajoo had a knowing smile on his lips. 'Are you not in love with Meena?'

Before replying, Kumar paced the floor. Then he went up to the camera crane lying, like a giant, in a corner. Finding some sort of support from fiddling with this steel contraption, he replied, 'People say that I fall in love with every heroine who appears in my films. There are also those who believe that I love only myself.'

'What do *you* say?' asked Rajoo, with an emphasis on the second person singular.

'I am in love—but not the kind of love that you or others imagine. For that love, I have my wife, my four adorable children. I'm in love with the great actress that lies within her, and who will come out one day before the world. But that will mean, for me, a lot of hard work, and for you ...'

'... a little sacrifice, isn't it?' Rajoo completed the sentence. Now he got up, having recovered his poise. He was master of himself. 'Kumar Saheb, you may be a great filmstar, but you don't know the character of a joker. No one can chain this two-legged shroud in trousers, as someone once described a poet. The joker is an eternal tramp and cannot be bound by gains of gold, or chains of love.' Then he walked up to Kumar, looked straight into his eyes. 'You are giving a new life to Meena. Remember that it is a big responsibility to take charge of someone's destiny.'

For a moment—just for a moment—Kumar could not but be moved by the intensity of Rajoo's emotion. But then he was the same practical-minded producer. 'By the way, in a few hours we are having Miss Meena's first press conference, when she will be presented to the world. You will come with her, I suppose.'

'I may or may not come,' said Rajoo. 'But Meena will reach you in time—and intact!'

Then, with a perfunctory '*namaste*', he turned and soon his footsteps on the studio floor could be heard receding in the distance.

Kumar watched him disappear, and murmured, 'Thanks, my friend.' Then he looked at the portraits of Meena, and kept looking at them for a long, long time. How beautiful she looked, how fresh and unspoilt! Suddenly a disturbing thought assailed him, 'Have I told Rajoo the truth? Or am I really falling in love with Meena?'

18

Meena, dressed in a silk sari and high-heeled sandals, at first did not recognize the slums when Rajoo stopped the taxi and asked her to accompany him.

'Where are you taking me?' she asked with obvious distaste at the odorous locality.

'Have you already forgotten Master Minoo and his heaven, for which he used to pay "nothing" as rent and where we used to eat "nothing", the favourite delicacy of our people, with great relish?'

When they had reached their old hut, it was still obviously untenanted, lying empty, desolate in disuse. There was dust and dirt everywhere, and across the door were cobwebs. Indeed, as they fought their way in, they found the whole place full of cobwebs.

'How filthy!' Meena squeezed her nose, taking out

her perfumed handkerchief. 'Cobwebs everywhere. Looks like a haunted house!'

'Yes, Meena,' said Rajoo, looking around for some old, familiar objects, 'it's haunted by old memories.'

'What are you talking about?' she asked impatiently. 'Why have you brought me here?'

'Meena, today you are entering a new life. I want you to take with you, in your heart, a memory of the hut. One day you may need it. It is good to look back at the dark valleys, when one approaches the summer of one's life.'

'But aren't you coming with me in this life?' She was obviously worried. 'What will I do without your help?'

'No, Meena, now you don't need my help. Now I'll see you on the silver screen—or should I say the technicolour screen—I'll be happy to be only your fan.'

'And what will *you* do?'

'For me only one door has been closed—all the other doors are still open. Don't you worry about me, Master Minoo. May I call you that, for once?'

Meena was nervous and fidgety as she fought back the surge of memories. Meanwhile, Rajoo saw that the old sari that he had once presented to her was lying in a discoloured heap, covered with dust and cobwebs. One end was still caught in a nail. Rajoo stretched the sari across the room.

'Look, Master Minoo, the sari has become a partition wall again.'

Meena kept silent, feeling ensnared in the cobwebs of the past.

She came out of her reverie with a start as she heard the sharp, urgent electric horn of the car sent by the studio to fetch her for the press conference.

'Go, Meena, or you'll be late. All the journalists and photographers are waiting to meet you.' Then, with a hollow chuckle, 'Don't forget to send me an invitation for the premiere of your first movie.'

Meena turned back from the door. 'You are sure you won't come with me? I need you.'

'No, Meena,' he replied. 'And remember one thing. As you go, don't look back. Neither today nor tomorrow.'

With an angry stamp of her sandalled foot, Meena walked out of the hut, brushing aside the cobwebs in the way, and walked straight out of the shanty town.

Now Rajoo was left alone. No, he had a companion—an old companion of his childhood, his youth.

It was the little joker that lay there, covered with dust caught in the cobwebs, left there by Meena who had once presumed to own it. Perhaps she had forgotten it. But then, was it not a fact that one forgot only what one subconsciously wanted to forget? Rajoo freed the little joker from the tangle of cobwebs, cleaned it, wiped the dust of the years from his face. Then he set it on the floor in front of him.

This little joker which was his own soul and self—he had tried to give away thrice—

first to Mary,

then to Marina,

then to Meena—

but every time it had been returned to him like a bad coin.

Today he had found the little joker amidst cobwebs, even as he had discovered himself caught in the cobwebs—

the cobwebs of love,

the cobwebs of desire,

the cobwebs of memory,

the cobwebs of frustration and loneliness.

He was caught in this flimsy web, spun out by a spider that was his own destiny. And caught up with him were memories—

the memory of Mary,

the memory of Marina,

the memory of Meena.

Meena, who had just gone away from here, gone away for good, never to return, never to look back, but the perfume of whose scented presence still lingered there among the dust and dirt and the cobwebs. Now she, too, was just a memory. Is memory, then, like a perfume? Does it linger only for a little while?

When tears welled up in his eyes he remembered what Mahender had told him years ago: 'No one should ever see tears in the eyes of a joker!' So he brought out the dark glasses, a parting gift from him, and put them on. Still the tears trickled down his cheeks.

He didn't know how long he continued to sit there, he did not even know what he was thinking—if he was thinking anything at all! His thoughts and his feelings became estranged from him; they wanted to leave him, to get out of that dirty, old hut, again and again seeking an escape. But there was no escape, for the cobwebs were everywhere; however high they might be, they were blocked by the web of the giant spider, 'destiny', as an old, old song reverberated through his consciousness.

'Where is Mary now?' he wondered.

'Where is Marina?'

'Where is Meena?'

Meena was being presented, in different glamorous costumes to set off her beauty, to the crowded press conference being held in a luxury hotel.

It was art and it was showmanship and it was business but, above all, it was an ego called Kumar which sought satisfaction in doing what no one had done before. Others had presented their heroines at press conferences, but he would outdo them all. So he had devised an elaborate fashion show, a revolving stage, a gorgeous, glamorous atmosphere, to provide the setting for the unveiling of his product, Meena—*his* discovery, *his* exclusive star, *his* property.

Along with the journalists were present a few select producers, too, Kumar's personal friends, and they all complimented him on his choice in superlative terms. Congratulations were pouring from all sides.

'Well done, Kumar, well done. You have a gold mine.'

'Thank you, thank you, what do you think of her?'

'Exquisitely beautiful. As for talent, let us wait and watch!'

'She needs only her beauty. Working with Kumar will bring out all the talent.'

When the press conference began, Meena, in a stunning white-and-silver ensemble, faced the journalists. The same old questions, but there were a few fresh answers.

'Miss Meena, when were you born?'

'Today—today I am born as a film artiste.'

The reporters noticed Meena's grateful look for Kumar.

'Miss Meena, what do you think about love?'

'Very dangerous—but very necessary for an artiste!'

Applause, laughter. 'Very good, Very clever, eh?'

'Who, above all others in your life, is responsible for your present success?'

For a few moments, Meena pondered the question before venturing a reply. She was looking at the cluster of lights focused on her, and seeing among them a glittering, gigantic cobweb in which Rajoo was caught, in which she herself was caught along with him, in which the tenderest and sweetest memories of her life were caught …

And now that palatial hotel, that glittering stage, that glamorous gathering, everything around her was slowly fading away into oblivion. But Meena remained as she was, the false smile frozen on her lips.

No longer was she at the press conference, but she was imprisoned in someone's heart, and that heart had splintered into a hundred fragments. And in each fragment of the heart, there was the same Meena smiling her false filmic smile.

Epilogue

NOT YET THE END!

As the wave of music swept up, the great show, starring the old joker, Rajoo, was still going on in the circus.

The fragile glass heart still lay splintered on the ground, and Rajoo—the old joker—was carefully, lovingly, collecting the fragments and loading them in a hand-cart, which he then painstakingly pushed out of the ring.

As he went out, hundreds of clowns, athletes, acrobats, handsome young men and beautiful young women, rushed in, singing and dancing—a great and resounding finale for the greatest show on earth. They were swaying to the rhythm of a familiar tune, singing in chorus—

Jeena yahaan, marna yahaan
Iske siwa jaana kahaan?

Singing with the chorus, his voice merged with the voice of the multitude, and the old joker returned to the centre with the dancers. He was now singing—

Kal khel mein hum ho na ho
Gardish mein taray rahengay sadaa

Bhoologe tum, bhoolengay woh,
Par hum tumharay rahengay sadaa.

(Tomorrow my game I may or may not play,
But in the sky the stars will remain forever,
You will forget and so, perhaps, shall they,
But yours I will remain forever.)

As he sang the last two lines, Rajoo, the old joker, looked in the direction where Mary and Marina and Meena were seated watching, fascinated, and next to them there were still some empty seats waiting for the guests to come—and for their memories of Rajoo!

Rajoo was now going up—and up—till he was high above the heads of all the other jokers and performers. Then, at a signal from him, the music and the singing was stilled, the circus arena was hushed into expectant silence, as he made an unusual announcement: 'Ladies and gentlemen. There will be an interval.' Then, looking at Marina, with a smile—'*Eto Entrakt* … This may be of fifteen minutes, as is usual, or fifteen hours, or fifteen months, but please don't go away. It is not yet the end of my story. The Joker's show is not yet over. Not yet …'

The circus resounded with thunderous applause. In the ring, hundreds of performers were singing, dancing, and Rajoo was singing with them, and the spectators were singing with Rajoo—for that moment, the performers and the spectators had become one, singing in unison, out of the unity of their hearts, of their emotions. In the centre, and high above the audience, stood Rajoo, the old joker, singing, urging people to sing louder, waving to his friends—and all were his friends. He was laughing and making the world laugh with him …

But, in the midst of this festival of gaiety and laughter, this colourful spectacle of song and dance, every now and then Rajoo's hand would go to his heart as his face contorted with unbearable pain—because his heart was too big, and the world too small!